To Harold L. Byers
See Dad, I told you...
d d

HORNY

S he liked his eyes. And not just the color, which she was sure all the other little girls had complimented him on to no end. She liked the fact they were open. They were wide open. They seemed to be taking in everything in a place where, up until she had seen him looking, she had been sure that there wasn't anything to see. He was with that asshole, Phil Flarn. And she wasn't sure she wanted to risk speaking to Phil Flarn just to chance an introduction. Then again, if she didn't speak to Phil, what were the chances they'd meet?

Decisions, decision…

"What's up, girl?" a voice came up behind her and she swelled into a hug that seemed as welcome and genuine as the sunrise. Luckily, she knew better. It was Alanda, her girl. Right, she thought to herself with wrinkled lips. She hadn't seen this bitch in a minute and, boy, did time fly!

"How you doin' lady?" Alanda asked. Quinn shrugged. *That good.* Alanda's quick flash of raised eyebrows seemed to imply an understanding. They stood there for a moment without speaking. Just nodding and looking at each other.

"Where is everybody?" Quinn asked finally.

"It's still early," Alanda said. Quinn caught Phil Flarn's

eye wandering towards her, frowning. Then just as quickly as he had looked, he looked away. She frowned.

"How's the album coming?" Alanda asked.

"It's coming," Quinn said, nodding unevenly and going into the self-imposed terror that always seemed to strike her whenever someone mentioned, inquired about, or seemed to even be thinking about her 'album'.

Suddenly, her shoulder seemed cold. She was wearing a red strapped tank in which her breasts hung heavy like pendulums and swayed with each step she took. She had known from the beginning when she had bought the tank that it would give her a bizarre combination of pride and shame for her upper half every time she put it on. Sure, she loved her heavy chest, the way her breasts seemed to be perfect, intimidating almost, but sometimes they were a burden. Sometimes they were a distraction. If she was making a point or voicing something she felt needed to be understood, they would be there seemingly mocking her seriousness. Lampooning her almost. However, if she simply wanted to be the sexiest thing in the room, there was nothing better than a pair of big, fat titties. The problem was, during the course of an evening she often wanted both sensations. To be taken in earnest and regarded as a hot sex object. Just what she wanted right then sent a chill through her shoulders. She rubbed her upper arms.

"What's up Quinn?" came a dull even tone from behind her. She turned and found herself face to face with an asshole: Phil Flarn.

"Phil," she said, hoping he would realize that by saying

nothing more she was neither greeting nor welcoming him. She was simply acknowledging that he was standing there and he had spoken.

"Seen my lady?" Phil asked monotone.

"She didn't come with you?" Quinn asked.

"Nah. I was supposed to meet her here. I brought my man with me."

Then *he* stepped forward.

"Quinn, this is Caesar," Phil said deftly. "Caese, this is Quinn."

"Nice to meet you," Caesar said a little unevenly and Quinn knew she liked him immediately.

"Nice to meet you too," she returned volley, looking into his eyes and deciding that, yes, she liked them for both reasons: their openness and their almost startling emerald and bronze coloring.

"I told her I was gonna be here at ten," Phil continued, returning to the issue of his missing girlfriend as he looked around the half-empty basement of a club. "She's probably somewhere with a dick in her mouth."

"Phil!" Quinn shouted, indignant.

"Goodness gracious," Caesar mumbled, trying to match Quinn's indignation but actually sounding just a little like he was really close to laughter.

"I mean, it's possible," Phil said, turning back around to face Quinn and smiling because he knew that he had got her. He had rattled her.

"But that's my girl. I'm not just gonna stand here and let you talk about my girl like that," Quinn defended.

"That's *my* girl," Phil corrected. "She's your friend.

She's only your girl if you're fuckin' her. You're not fuckin' her, are you?"

"Yes," Quinn deadpanned. "I'm fucking her."

"I knew it," Phil snapped. "I knew y'all was into that shit! All you jazz bitches are alike. From now on I'm only fuckin' with hip-hop bitches."

Before Quinn had a chance to load up and return, Phil was gone, disappearing into a conversation with a bass player they both knew.

Quinn watched him, unaware that she was shaking her head and also unaware that he had left something behind with her.

"He was only saying that to bother you."

She stared up at him, up into his beautiful eyes.

"That your *friend?*" she asked hotly, ready to see how he got down.

"All my life," he said quickly.

He had defended his friend, despite the fact that it probably wouldn't get him any points with her. She liked that.

"Why does he do that to people?" she asked, now simply trying to understand how an obvious lunatic like Phil Flarn could have someone like this pretty-eyed boy come to his defense.

"I don't know," Caesar said frowning. "I think he likes you, though. If he didn't, he wouldn't have anything to say to you at all."

Quinn nodded, thinking that if insults were the price of Phil's friendship she'd just as soon be his enemy.

"Does he talk to you like that?"

"Never," Caesar said.

"Why, doesn't he like you?" she asked coyly.

"Nope," Caesar said shaking his head. "He loves me."

"There is a difference," Quinn breezed.

"There is a difference," Caesar acknowledged.

"Dyke bitch!" came a scream at the other end of the room. Both Quinn and Caesar knew without looking up that it was Phil doing the screaming and that Joyce must have just walked in.

"How could you do this to me?" the screaming continued. "I loved you woman!"

Caesar continued to look at Quinn. Even though Quinn was still watching the action, she could feel his eyes on her. She watched from the distance as Joyce descended the stairs, then leapt into the waiting arms of that asshole: Phil Flarn. They kissed like they were alone. Then Joyce screamed.

"Who you callin' a dyke?" It was a high, loud shriek.

"Faggot-ass nigga," Joyce continued. "You don't want me to let everybody in here know about that little thing you got for Kobe Bryant."

Phil looked terrified. "You said you'd keep that between us," he pleaded.

Some people didn't get it.

Quinn shook her head. *There but for the grace of God...* she thought.

Phil and Joyce were walking hand in hand until they disappeared behind a pillar and were gone. When Quinn turned around, she was again face to face with Caesar. She was happy that he'd remained, but suddenly she didn't know what to say.

"You know Joyce, right?" he asked, breaking the ice before it had a chance to fully form.

"That's my girl," Quinn said quickly.

"I like her and Phil as a couple," Caesar said.

Quinn gritted her teeth, unsure of what she was expected to say next. It wasn't that she didn't like Joyce and Phil as a couple. It was that she didn't like Phil. Phil made anything bad. He could have carried the instruments for Miles Davis and them back during the *Kind of Blue* recordings and Quinn was sure that the album would have in some way turned out different. It would have turned out wrong. Phil was a hell of a piano player, though. She had to give him that. And he was making one of her best friends happy. And he was here with this pretty-eyed boy.

"I guess I do too," Quinn said finally.

Caesar nodded, happy to have hurdled that obstacle and only then, for the first time, did Quinn catch him looking at the other two between them.

"You like those?" she asked smiling.

"Oh my God..." he moaned as she burst out laughing hysterically. "I mean..." he continued before pausing, "I don't wanna be rude or anything, but those are incredible."

Quinn grabbed them, cupping her hands beneath and squeezing, causing the already visible area of cleavage to swell in front of her.

"They're just titties," she said simply.

"That's like saying a Benz is just a car," he moaned as she laughed. "Or Ali is just fighter," he continued as she laughed some more. "Or a diamond's just a rock," he concluded, giving her a chance to moan.

"I think I like you," she said as she regarded him with a slanted eye. "You know how to make a girl feel good."

"And I ain't even do nothin' yet," he said quickly.

"Quinn," came a male voice from behind her.

She turned, distracted, ready to end quickly whatever interference was going to keep her from talking at length to this pretty-eyed boy.

It was Shaun. He was lunging across the floor towards her like he had something on his mind to let off. Quinn steadied herself.

"What's up, baby?" he asked, leaving way too much of his open mouth on her cheek as he kissed and made sure to sweep a backhand across her chest as he moved to hug her.

"Hello Shaun," she said flatly.

"Look baby," Shaun began, "you got any songs on you?"

Quinn frowned.

"I know what you're thinking," Shaun continued quickly. "But we're in the studio right now and we need two more songs to choose from before we pick the final twelve for the album."

"So what? You want me to come up with one for you right now?"

Shaun made his 'cute' face. The face he made whenever he thought he might have to use his sex appeal as part of an extra incentive. Somebody should have told him.

"You don't have to write one if you got one," he said in

his best FM radio DJ's voice, leaning with his fleshy body towards her as if hoping the top of his stomach might somehow graze the bulk of the bottom of her titties. Quinn leaned away.

She had actually liked Shaun at one point. Thought he was cool. He was a good enough producer, able to collect some of the most talented young musicians around and get them to play together without egos. His ego had been his only problem. He doubled as a bass player and lately he'd been forgetting about his day job. He had actually begun to believe that he'd become a talented enough bass player with a big enough following to sell records.

He'd been pressuring people lately to play and sing on a new album that he was producing, featuring himself. Now, as he stood in front of her, his yellow skin seemed effective in only making him look sick. His gut was neatly packaged in his black jeans and camouflaged in his black Nike sweatshirt and a black beret which made him look like some impossible cross between Charles Mingus and Huey P. Newton. Quinn didn't know which insulted her more; that he was only coming to her now to participate in his album, or that he was only asking her to come up with a song and not sing.

"How much is it worth to you?" Quinn asked, deadpan.

Shaun looked as if she had called his mother a country and western singer.

"Why would you insult me like that?" he asked, trying his best to seem hurt. "You know I'm gonna give you scale."

"Scale?" Quinn asked, incredulous. "For a song come

up with right now? Forget it," she said waving him away. "I'll starve."

"How much do you want then?" he asked simply.

"Five percent of the gross royalties," she said simply.

"From the song?" he asked too eagerly. He had no intent of making the song a single.

"From the album," she said. Shaun's eyes grew wide.

"It's only gonna be one song on an album of twelve," Shaun cried.

"That's why I'm only asking for five percent," Quinn said simply. Shaun looked thoughtful.

"Alright," he began. "But for that kind of money, I want 'Lover Man'." Before her eyes had a chance to grow to full wattage, he added, "And I want you to sing it."

"Un-uh," Quinn shook her head with her mouth open. "Shaun, you know I've been saving that song for my album."

"What album?" Shaun asked cruelly. "Girl, you been making an album since I've known you and ain't an album come out yet."

How could she explain it to him? Better yet, how could she make him understand? The fact that her album hadn't come out wasn't her fault. She was working on it even as they spoke.

"Twenty thousand up front," a voice said from deep inside her. Her hand was actually covering her mouth. It was as if she was whispering it to herself, but in her speaking voice. She listened again for the voice but it didn't come. She seemed startled when she looked at Shaun.

"Twenty-thousand up front?!?" he cried out.

"And five points," the voice said quickly.

"Now wait a minute," Shaun said, raising a hand.

"That's what I want," the voice said.

There was a pause.

Quinn wasn't mad at this voice. She just wanted to know where it was coming from. For twenty thousand dollars, she could do a lot of things.

"And five points," the voice said again as Quinn nodded her head.

"Quinn…" Shaun pleaded.

Quinn shook her head. Then nodded again.

"Come by the studio later tonight…" Shaun exhaled.

For the second time that night Quinn was actually happy. She watched Shaun walk away and began to look around the party. It wasn't that crowded. Most of the revelers were jazz or music people and it amazed her how they all looked alike. The men all looked like rappers, bank robbers or poets. Except for the older guys. And there were few of those. She looked at the women, some as bold as jeans and boots, others in wraps and headwraps. Hip-hop was playing and it amazed her that some of the people in the party seemed to know the song. She watched the heads boppin' and as people scampered towards the dance floor she was struck with the sudden desire to laugh. That's Biggie Smalls, she thought. Do those people know that? She did, hip-hop head that she was, and fought with her own tongue to keep private. These people, she had always thought, would never understand. Hip-hop was supposed to be a bastard. She was the product of a good family: jazz.

Well, at least, that's how some jazz people carried it. Some made it seem like there was nothing of substance except jazz. Every other music was of a poor father. And hip-hop, of course, had no father. But there they were, jumping all around to the one song she knew of where the late Notorious B.I.G. and the late Tupac Shakur collaborated. And the DJ kept playing the part where Biggie's caught up chanting rhetorically:

WHERE BROOKLYN AT?

WHERE BROOKLYN AT?

WHERE BROOKLYN AT?

WHERE BROOKLYN AT?

Just as suddenly, Quinn's eyes narrowed. What had been the first thing that had made her happy that night, she wondered, remembering that the deal with Shaun was the second. It was certainly not the goosebumps. Her breasts grew hot, which meant that somebody was looking at them. She didn't search out the intruder. Instead she focused on trying to remember what had made her happy. Then she heard a voice.

"Hey Quinn," Joyce was screaming at her.

Quinn was happy to see her. She wasn't happy to see what Joyce was dragging.

"We seen each other. We seen each other!" Phil Flarn protested. His fingers were in the vice grip that was Joyce's right hand.

"You saw Phil?" Joyce asked.

Quinn nodded. Joyce released Phil Flarn. He ran off.

Quinn found herself watching that asshole: Phil Flarn. Carefully. He headed towards the back of the converted basement that was serving as the party facility, to the bar, then stopped. He made a right and headed towards the back steps where there were two bathrooms and several opportunistic young men selling marijuana and Ecstasy tablets. He disappeared past them.

When she turned her eyes straight, Joyce was still standing there talking. Thankfully she was able to pick up the conversation. But now she remembered what had first made her happy that night.

Now it made her sad. The pretty-eyed boy was gone.

Caesar Brown was on his way to work. He worked at night. All night at a hospital. In the laboratory, analyzing bacteria and shit. He wasn't no doctor or anything. Didn't wanna be. His job just paid the bills. He had a daughter to take care of and a mom (if anybody can ever really take care of their parents). Caesar was always searching his brain for angles. Tonight had been a good night, he thought, as his tires touched the Manhattan side of the Brooklyn Bridge and he began on his way to the West Side Highway. Phil Flarn had been himself, which was always good for some laughs if nothing. He also got a chance to see Joyce again. And he had met a girl.

He hadn't wanted to be rude the way that that dude had been. That light-skinned dude with the gut that had intruded right as he was about to try and get the number. Besides, he didn't know the dude or the dude's relationship with Quinn. He tried to wait her out, but she took too long. He had to get to work. His only hope was that Phil Flarn seemed to know her. She didn't seem to like

Phil Flarn, but nobody ever seemed to like Phil Flarn. She might like me though, Caesar thought to himself with a nod. Yeah, she might like me, he thought again.

Quinn had settled into a chair facing a small table that was bolted to the ground. Booths lined the wall to her right, pretty much filled with people who had already gathered into their cliques and now sat talking and studying other cliques. Quinn looked up and watched the wanderers flowing in and out of several cliques, getting the whole experience. The boys in dreds were killing her. She remembered how she had loved the style when it was new and fresh and rebellious. It was like that with everything, she imagined. She thought about Afros. Before Afros had become a staple they had been a statement. Their first wearers were revolutionaries. She remembered how black hairstyles took a break from politics during the jheri curl era, then came back with basketball players and bald heads. Then those too became standards. Dreds had always been beautiful, but now even those were becoming neutral. She wondered how long cornrows would last before kids would be wearing them in commercials to sell soda pop.

The DJ lost all the respect he might have gained from the Biggie/Tupac collaboration when, immediately after, he threw on 'Before I Let Go' by Frankie Beverly and Maze. It seemed as if he was gunning for everybody, but in a haphazard way. Even people that might have wanted to hear 'Before I Let Go' certainly didn't want to hear it right after Biggie, and responded with one unanimous moan.

Quinn was smiling now and talking as somebody walked up and took her hand. She knew the face. She didn't wanna work hard enough to remember the name. She wanted to leave, but it was too early to meet Shaun in the studio. She wanted an emotion because she was selling what she believed to be the best song she'd ever written. She wanted some Ecstasy.

She got up from her chair and walked, smiling and nodding, speaking when necessary as she passed people. She made it to the back where the boys were. She knew some of them. She was looking for one. He was there, with his dreds, by the men's bathroom on the second floor. She didn't speak to him, she just tilted her head to the side and handed him the rumpled twenty and five-dollar bills, and he dug into his pocket rather obviously and pulled out the off-white pill in a small, clear plastic bag. She rushed downstairs in search of a beer. She was sipping and on her way back to her seat before she popped the pill. No one had taken her seat. She was so thankful she could have cried.

It was a while before she felt the first rush, paranoid as she always was with everything: What if it doesn't work? What if it's not Ex? What if it kills me? But when she suddenly loved that asshole: Phil Flarn, she knew it was working. Phil Flarn was beautiful. He was being good to her girl Joyce. That was cool. The world was beautiful. You could do beautiful things in it. God was beautiful...

Quinn sat with her arms crossed. It occurred to her that her hands were very near her breasts. She wanted to touch them. She debated for a moment, thinking of the club and the people in it and considering how they would feel to watch her touch herself so lovingly in their presence. So she decided to be private and turn a little to her right so that anybody noticing her touching her breasts would have to be looking at her so hard that they deserved whatever guilt or pleasure they derived from watching.

Her breasts were huge. She thanked God for that right then. She should have never complained. She ran her hands along her hips. Her hips were slim. She thanked God for that right then. She should have never complained. She touched her face. Her face was smooth. She thanked God for that right then. She should have never complained…

She was enjoying herself. Loving herself. Loving God. Loving life. Loving. She had just sold what she believed to be the best song she'd ever written and she loved it. That song would be on an album that people would buy. That song would be heard. And she would be the one explaining it. She wanted to sing right then but the DJ, God bless him, and his inability to keep a flow going, was playing 'The Candy Man' by Sammy Davis Jr and part of her wanted to cry. She wasn't sad. It was that the heaviness of all the love was becoming too much for her and she had to let it out somehow.

It was with all this in mind that she floated into the studio later that night. Shaun didn't like the look on her face. The players all had their game faces on. This was work. And here she came looking happy.

"Y'all ready?" she asked, walking right up to the mic and standing before it waiting for some sort of signal that she could begin. All these dudes knew the music. They were pros. Shaun looked at the technician and shrugged. The technician nodded to Shaun. He nodded unevenly to Quinn. She began to sing. When she was finished, her head sunk into her chest and she left.

"One take," she heard Shaun's astounded voice proclaiming over her shoulder as she walked towards the door. "One mothafuckin'…"

She closed the door.

The wind and night greeted Quinn like a friend. She wondered about a cab, a car, and a way home. She thought about walking all the way back home watching the lights of lower Manhattan glow from the Brooklyn Bridge in the middle of winter, . A cooler wind, different from the friend that had greeted her at the door, changed her plans and, before she knew it, her hand was extended towards an ugly yellow motorized bug with four wheels, four doors and a foreign guy driver.

"Fort Greene," she said to the cab driver, her voice reminding her of a woman she had heard singing somewhere moments before.

"Take the Manhattan Bridge," she said before he asked.

The backseat smelled of stale humanity. She wondered what combination of life had produced such a smell. Were they white men coming from Chelsea Piers, thoroughly convinced that given what they could do now plus the advantages of youth, they might have really been able to become professional athletes? Were they white women fresh from a sale, deodorant and perfume now a memory and full of the funk that comes from shopping as an indoor sport? Were they young brothas that moved quickly and, therefore, had little time for stuff like cleanliness beyond the customary simplicity of a shower a day? Were they sistas like herself, keeping the cab from completely stinking, but unable to make the smell totally pleasant either because of the smallness of their numbers? Quinn smiled as she thought that she was probably contributing one of the better smells to the cab, thinking about the next passenger and how, if that person knew what she was doing for them simply by being, they would thank her. And she would thank them, she thought, as she swerved back under the Ecstasy influence. Because God made them all. And God bless them all. Everyone.

The numbers on the alarm clock were red and fuzzy. They said 11am. They were lying. They had to be. If they were telling the truth, then she was late. And if she was late again, she just might not have any place to go. She smacked her hand across the nightstand in search of the phone. She found it after patting down the alarm clock, an old used condom wrapper, Alice Walker's *Temple of My Familiar*, and a Last Poets CD. She called the office.

"Big Niggaz?" answered Carmen.

"Bill come in yet?" Quinn asked, her voice sounding nothing like the voice she remembered from the night before.

"Quinn, where are you, girl?" Carmen asked.

"Home," Quinn said simply.

"Well, you installin' a cash register in your bathtub or you coming in?" Carmen mocked, her voice slipping into the light Latina accent that she saved only for people she felt comfortable with.

"I'm coming," Quinn said, smiling at Carmen's overdone accent. The girl's parents were Dominican. She was born in New Jersey. "If Bill comes in just tell him that I went out to get a sandwich or something."

"Will do, Ma-Ma," Carmen cheered.

Quinn was in a pair of jeans before she had even looked at herself. A sleeveless T-shirt of Life's lay crumpled across the sofa. She put it on, followed by a Big Niggaz button down. There was a Big Niggaz baseball cap on the bathroom doorknob. She put it on before even attempting to look at her hair. Then she checked the mirror. It looked like her. Just not a her that she'd want to mess with if she was a guy meeting her for the first time. Didn't matter, she thought with a shrug. That was the her that she was giving the world today. And if the world didn't want it, they could always give it back.

She took the train into the city as always, slightly put off by the fact that her ordinary to-work crew was nowhere to be found. The group that she saw each morning when she was on time to work. The group that she could count on to be waiting for the same car in the train, and the group that she could count on to be already seated in that car when it came. That group had already gone to work. On time, Quinn imagined. This was a different group, she thought as she looked around on the platform and again as she climbed into the second to last car on the C train. Who knew where these people were going or what their story was? They were probably thinking the same thing about her, she thought as she watched them stare for a while, then finally tiring of them, responding by opening a magazine.

Before she knew it, Quinn had reached her stop and was out among people headed to early lunches and possibly even illicit affairs, judging by the pure goofiness with which some of them carried themselves. Why were so many people in this part of Manhattan, this no man's land between the West and East villages, this above-Soho NYU area wasteland, she wondered as she watched grunge band lookalikes parade past with their dyed-black and thoroughly pierced girlfriends in tow. She shook off the thought. Post-Ex pessimism, she told herself.

"Oh Mami," Carmen greeted as Quinn used what seemed to be the last of her strength to push open the door. "Lettin' it all hang out."

Quinn looked from Carmen's eyes to where they were resting and then she realized; she wasn't wearing a bra.

"God…" Quinn moaned.

"Not only will Bill not wanna fire you," Carmen began. "He might even wanna give you a raise."

"I didn't do this on purpose…" Quinn began weakly.

"Why you worried?" Carmen asked. "If you got it, flaunt it. I ain't got what you got up top," she said as she pushed out her B-cups as far as she could, "but you better believe I work my biggest asset."

With that, Carmen turned to reveal the latest incarnation of her behind: Carmen's ass in tight black satin. The sight of it even made Quinn's chest a little warm.

"Girl, you're crazy," Quinn said, unable to remove her eyes, which she knew was exactly Carmen's intention.

"*Girl, you look good,*" Carmen began singing, "*better back that ass up…*" and with that she gripped her own hips and thrust them backwards towards Quinn.

Quinn shook her head and walked to the back of the store.

"Busy?" she asked, beginning to adjust the sweater on a

mannequin where it was hanging wrong.

"A couple of white boys came in and bought cargo pants," Carmen said.

"Different styles?"

Carmen shook her head.

"The same exact pair," she said.

Quinn shook her head.

Quinn was thinking about how when she heard that Bill Pryor was starting a clothing line she had smirked. Niggas was always doing something crazy as she saw it. Particularly niggas that were known for doing something else. Bill Pryor was already a success. He made movies Francis Ford Coppola-style with black people in all the lead roles. By the time he had announced that he was coming out with a clothing line, he had made *The Godmother I* and *II*, *The Rap*, *Apocalypse Soon*, and had begun working on *The Godmother III*. In the meantime, he had also come out with a clothing line that was to be named after something that he was sure everybody aspired to be: a large negro. When Quinn had heard the name of the line, she had vomited. Now she worked for the man.

It was funny really, the way she had approached him that day on the street hoping only for some light on the next soundtrack he was due to release.

"Lemme hear you sing," he had said dubiously.

She remembered him frowning after she had finished. This actually wasn't anything new. Everybody seemed to frown the first time they heard her sing. Nobody even knew what to make of something the likes of which they had never heard.

"We should stay in touch," he had said that day on the street and with that, gave her a business card. When she got fed up with her old job selling advertising space in the newspaper and decided to spend all her time trying to launch her singing career, she called Bill Pryor aggressively. He deferred her just as aggressively. Finally, one day she just broke down and told him, "Look, I'm broke. I quit my job. I need work." She remembered the heavy silence on the other end of the phone, the audible exhale, then his voice.

"Well, you be the manager at the shop I'm opening up for my indie clothing line," he said.

"You want me to be a Big Nigga?" she asked.

"Hey, you're starving, not me," he said with just a little bit of edge creeping into his tone.

She agreed and started working the next Monday morning.

When Bill finally did show up that day, there had been no evidence of how late Quinn had been. Or so she thought.

"What time'd you get here?" he asked in a low tone, having sneaked up behind her and almost startled her with his voice.

"A while ago," she said deadpan.

"That's not an answer," he said.

"It's the only one I got," she said. When she turned, he was walking away, headed upstairs to his film offices. She turned to face Carmen, whose eyes were already on her.

"I don't think he'd fire you," Carmen said.

"I don't think he wouldn't," Quinn said in return.

Carmen nodded silent. Quinn liked her. So much that she never let on to people that knew them both that Carmen's 'Dominican Mami' thing was just a front. Carmen was Dominican all right, but she was as far from the Washington Heights-type character that she liked to play, as Garth Brooks was from Tito Puente. The girl was all white bread. Born and raised in Englewood, New Jersey. Educated in Catholic schools all her life before moving to the city to attend Columbia. Carmen was beautiful and it was more than just the mixture of African, Indian and Spanish influences on her lineage. Her eyes were always wide with awe and her lips permanently curled as if she had just said the most important thing she'd ever say. Her hair had a straight but thick, almost Asian, quality. And her skin was a little darker than the caramel inside a Snickers bar. She wasn't too tall, which was probably for the best because her ass would have looked ridiculous on a taller girl. And she was funny. When she had first started at Big Niggaz and Quinn didn't know what to make of her, they were well into a conversation about how to price the T-shirts when Quinn heard what sounded like, "Pretty smart: for a cotton picker."

"What did you say?" Quinn had whirled around to demand.

"I said you're pretty smart," Carmen said, looking at her supervisor incredulously. After Quinn nodded and turned back around, the words "For a cotton picker," were in her ears again.

"Bitch, are you crazy?" Quinn had demanded.

"Why you callin' me a bitch?" Carmen had demanded, sounding genuinely offended.

"Why are you callin' me a cotton picker?" Quinn demanded.

"Cause that's what you are," Carmen had said simply.

Quinn paused, searching for logic.

"Why, you Spanish-Haitian bitch…" but before she could finish, she had to frown and wonder what on earth this crazy Dominican girl was laughing about.

"What's so funny?" Quinn asked, not sure whether or not she should be mad.

"Spanish-Haitian," she giggled. "That's good. I was wondering what you really thought about me. Now we can be friends."

All Quinn could do was shake her head. They were friends.

Carmen was the only person that had actually swooned the first time she heard Quinn sing.

"You sing so beautiful," she had said with those eyes so wide that a lie would have had no place to hide.

"Thank you," Quinn had said simply, unable to think of anything else to say. Appreciation always meant a lot to her.

Carmen had this crazy boyfriend. His name was Steeze. He was Dominican, of course. From Washington Heights, which Quinn knew in Carmen's book was a bigger plus than if he'd been from the Dominican Republic itself. There was nothing more 'real' to a Jersey Dominican than a Dominican from Washington Heights.

Steeze worked at a record company and whenever he was around, Carmen became vicariously crazy. Her eyes would grow even wider and she seemed to be eager or willing to do anything that Steeze suggested. Quinn wondered exactly what that was sometimes, for whenever she and Steeze had a conversation he always ended up talking to her breasts.

"What the deal Quinn?" he would ask her titties.

"Same ol', Steeze," she'd say, then duck to meet his eyes. It would never work. His eyes would follow her titties even lower.

When Quinn saw Steeze hopping through his high walk into the store that day, her titties got hot instinctively. She knew they'd be the star of at least the next several moments.

"What's up, baby?" he asked, smiling like he'd won money when he saw Carmen's eager face.

Carmen was hopping in place.

"Hey baby!" She screamed like she hadn't just seen the man that morning. They embraced, her wrapping her arms around his neck, him wrapping his left arm around her waist and using his right hand led by his middle finger to dig low into the cleft in her pants separating her ass-cheeks and slowly dragging his hand to the top of her butt.

Steeze was looking over his girlfriend's shoulder when he spotted Quinn. He smiled and motioned with his head to her. She smirked and motioned back. He broke his embrace with Carmen and walked to the back of the store. Quinn braced herself. And her titties.

"When you, me, Carmen and your man Life gonna get

together and go out?" he asked her titties when he reached
where she was folding a pair of jeans with cargo pants
pockets.

"I don't have a man," Quinn said deadpan.

"You and Life ain't together no more?" he asked,
staring at her titties.

"Un-uh," Quinn said, shaking her head.

Steeze twisted his lips and shook his head.

"So when's the last time that you got fucked?" he
asked. And even though Quinn started to speak, the
thought that stopped her was that he was looking at her
titties. What if he was asking her titties?

"Steeze!" Carmen screamed from the front of the store.
"That's personal. She might not wanna tell you that."

Quinn chuckled against her will.

"So what's the deal?" Steeze asked. "You wanna tell
me?"

Quinn took a deep breath and exhaled.

"A couple of nights ago," the words came, shocking
even Quinn as she heard them.

"Was it Life?" Steeze asked.

"Yeah," Quinn exhaled.

"Well at least he's still good for something."

With that he turned and started walking back to
Carmen.

"I'ma fuck this girl tonight, baby," he said, putting his
arm around Carmen's shoulder.

Carmen nodded unevenly.

"Guess I'll find somebody to fuck," she said through an
exhale. "You gonna do oral?"

Steeze shook his head.

"Straight sex," he said simply. "Probably all Missionary Position."

Carmen nodded.

"Would you mind if I got it from the back?" she asked.

Steeze leaned his head a little to the side. He looked thoughtful.

"Is it gonna be somebody new?" he asked.

"Probably," she said. "Is your girl new?"

Steeze nodded.

"Then yeah," Carmen said.

"I guess," Steeze said with a reluctant shrug. "Long as his dick's not, like, huge, and he can fuck you from across the street or some shit."

Against her will, Quinn burst out laughing.

"Could you imagine that?" Steeze asked, now speaking to Quinn. "I'd have to hear it from one of my niggas or some shit. 'Yo Steeze, I saw your girl getting fucked by this big-dick nigga and shit. He was fucking her from the apartment next door'."

Quinn was hysterical.

"That's why you stayed with Life so long, wasn't it?" Steeze asked. "Nigga ain't had no job. No college education. No prospects."

Quinn was still laughing.

"Nigga must have been able to fuck you from across the street facing in the opposite direction."

Everybody started laughing. Even Bill who had come downstairs to grab a T-shirt. Everybody else stopped laughing when they noticed Bill.

"How ya doin', Mr. Pryor?" Steeze said with mock reverence. "When you gonna let me do the soundtrack to one of your films?"

"Steeze," Bill began tiredly, "you have some of the most no-talented rappers I've ever heard."

"That's not true," Steeze interrupted hotly. "We just signed this kid from Newark, he spits nothing but pure fire."

"That's what you said about MC Nursery," Bill said flatly.

"Who knew those were Old Mother Goose and Dr Seuss rhymes?" Steeze defended.

"Somebody at your label should have," Bill said. "It would have saved you guys a twenty million dollar lawsuit."

"Listen," Steeze began earnestly. "Let me let you hear the demo for this kid from Newark we got. His name is Turtle Wax…"

"Uh-oh," Bill interrupted to moan.

"No, listen," Steeze continued earnestly, "his name is Turtle Wax because he waxes other MCs. See, he raps fast and most other MCs rap slow. That's why he calls other MCs 'turtles'. He calls them 'turtles' and he waxes them."

Bill could do nothing but shake his head.

"Just let me let you hear him," Steeze beseeched.

Bill looked skeptical.

"You got the demo on you?" he asked.

"Of course," Steeze said, merrily pulling a C-90 from his front pants pocket. He tossed it across the store to Bill. Bill caught it on the fly.

"All right," Bill said reluctantly. "But if this guy's a bum, I never wanna hear about another 'artist' that you guys are putting out."

Steeze smiled and nodded excitedly.

"Just play the tape," he said confidently. "You'll see."

Bill nodded unconvincingly and turned, heading back up the stairs.

"Yeah," Steeze cheered, motioning with his right arm as if he had just thrown a touchdown pass.

Quinn liked Steeze. He was a sexy boy. She'd catch herself watching his Dominican ass and wonder if he moved the way he did because he knew she was watching, or if he was just naturally that hot. She liked his clothes and the way he accessorized, nothing in a pattern. He wore hats sometimes and sunglasses or scarves and knit hats. The ruggedest boots sometimes or the most faggotty sneakers. He wore whatever was on his mind.

"You should fuck him," Carmen had said one day. "He's good."

It had caught Quinn as a shock because that particular day, she had been watching him as usually and totally lost track of Carmen. It wasn't like her to be like that. To be disrespectful. Watching another woman's man, much less right in front of the woman. But then Carmen suggested she fuck him. Right there in her ear.

"Why would you want me to fuck your man?" Quinn asked. She wanted to know.

"Cause he's good," Carmen said simply.

Quinn was silent.

Sure, she'd have liked to fuck Steeze, for the action. The

emotion was something she didn't want to deal with. The trauma, perhaps, of her and Carmen both knowing that Quinn had fucked her man. How would that affect them when they were alone together or whenever Steeze came around? That was the part she didn't want to have to deal with.

"What would you get out of this?" Quinn asked. She wanted more answers.

"Could I fuck Life?" Carmen asked, interest growing in her eyes.

"You wanna fuck my boyfriend?" Quinn asked incredulously.

"Sure," Carmen cheered. "Don't you?"

Again, Quinn was silent. There were three thoughts running through her head. Carmen wanted to have sex with her boyfriend. She wanted to have sex with Steeze. And there was a deal on the table.

"What kind of relationship do y'all have?" Quinn forced herself to ask.

"Open," Carmen said simply.

"I would imagine..." Quinn said.

Carmen laughed.

"I'm gonna be with Steeze the rest of my life," she began, as serious as Quinn had ever seen her. "He's not finished fucking around yet. So what should I do? Should I wait for him to finish and punish myself by not being with him now? Should I leave him now and punish myself by not being with him later? Or should I just stay with him and do what he does?"

"Those can't be the only choices?" Quinn frowned.

"Gimme some others," Carmen demanded.

"Tell him to stop fucking around."

"What if he says 'no'?"

"Then don't give him any."

"He's already getting some. He's fucking around, remember?"

Quinn was silent.

"Then leave him," she said.

"I don't want to."

Quinn was silent.

"Then just stay with him and just..." she searched her mind for solutions. "Listen," she began again, "just because he's fucking around don't mean you got to. You could have some respect for your body."

"Respect for my body?" Carmen asked, her eyes bordering on incredulous.

"Yeah, you don't have to be using your body like that," Quinn said.

"Scuse me," Carmen began, breaking into her stereotype. "Respecting my body means using my body any way that I want to, thank you. And not letting it be misused by others."

Right then there was a large pop of bubble gum in Carmen's mouth. Quinn, up until that point, hadn't noticed that she was even chewing gum.

"So y'all both fuck around?" Quinn asked slowly.

"Sure, why should he have all the fun?"

"Do you guys tell each other about these experiences?"

"Sure. He makes sure he tells me who had bigger titties than me. He knows it fucks with me. So I make sure to tell him who has a bigger dick than he does. He acts like it doesn't bother him, but I know it does."

Quinn glanced at Steeze who, at the time, was standing and listening to Bill explain how to write screenplays. He was sexy even listening.

"That's why you should fuck him," Carmen said, catching Quinn again. "He wants to fuck you anyway. You got them big-ass titties. That's the only thing I don't got. He'll probably wanna tittie fuck you. You'll like his dick. You should suck it and everything."

"And what would you be doing with Life?" Quinn asked, eyes widening.

Carmen shrugged.

"It depends," she said. "How big is his dick?"

Every day Quinn wrote a song. She wrote a song to music in her mind. She sang it in her mind and wrote it on paper hoping that the way she wrote the words would remind her how she had sung the song. She had sold a couple of songs. She was getting into that a little now. In the beginning, she had been hesitant to sell songs because she wanted to use every song she had written herself. Nobody could ever sing any of her songs like her. She was the one that had felt it. Eventually though, with money getting lower and art and shit beginning to mean a lot less than rent and shit, she began selling songs for a flat rate. By this time she had figured that if she could write a song, she could write another song. She figured that what was important was not as much that she deliver the message but that the message got out there. She figured that the people she sold the songs to would be fools to tamper with the perfection she had given them, but if so, so be it. She also needed the money. She thought about her career. Her life. Her life wasn't her career, of course. Her career wasn't even her life. They were just these two things that kept bumping into each other at the most unfortunate of times, each vying for supremacy and acting like brats. She didn't complain or whine, but her life did. She wasn't a tease and a disappointment, but her career was. Nothing was wrong with her. The world was at fault. And she had to work hard to make it right. This was how she thought. She couldn't wait to sing. That would heal so many people, she figured. The way Aretha Franklin had healed her. The way Marvin Gaye had and Nina Simone. The way Diana Ross had and Etta James. The way Sarah Vaughn had. That was what she'd do for people, when she got a chance.

The song wasn't coming today. Neither was the music. But she would have to write a song. She couldn't sleep unless she had written a song. She was lying in bed, eyes wide. Her living room light was on, casting a shadow into her room. The oatmeal colored walls made her hungry. Maybe that's what she needed, food, she thought as she sat upright. Did she have any? Watermelon, she thought. *Why watermelon?* Why not watermelon? She stood up and floated to the kitchen, a song refusing to come. She reached for the refrigerator door as the alarm went off.

As she watched the clock, walking across the room towards the phone, she wondered who on earth would be calling. It was Joyce.

"Yeah, I remember him," Quinn said.

Joyce had asked if she remembered the guy who had been with that asshole: Phil Flarn, the night before at the party. Caesar, the boy with the pretty eyes.

"Well, he asked Phil how to get in contact with you," Joyce said through the phone. "Do you want him to get in contact with you?"

"Where's Phil?" Quinn asked, hearing nothing but Joyce's voice through the phone, and finding it impossible to imagine that asshole: Phil Flarn not making himself evident in the background.

"He's here," Joyce said. "You wanna talk to him or something?"

Apprehension filled Quinn.

"No," she said perhaps a little too quickly. She thought about the pretty-eyed boy.

"Well," Quinn began again, "tell Phil that he can give Caesar my number."

"Okay," Joyce said, simply enough. She hung up.

Quinn forgot about the watermelon as she got up and walked back into her bedroom. She lay back down and looked at the light in the living room again. It was funny. She knew that the real chick had actually dated a white dude named Marc Anthony but for some reason, she had always linked her to the Roman emperor Caesar. That's why when the music came on in her head and the words started coming to her, 'Be Your Cleopatra' became the song's title even though the lyrics were historically incorrect.

Life was inside of her and she couldn't say she wasn't enjoying it. She needed it, she told herself. A reward for just being able to keep her sanity. The guilt and other things that played with her she kept barricaded back, back against the back of her mind. She didn't wanna think about anything but the action. She didn't even wanna think about the protagonists. Then Life came, abruptly, surprising the shit out of her and seemingly out of himself as well. She became real; a person taking part in what was

going on around her. She wanted to go back to the action.
But that was over.

"Damn, Life," she moaned.

"What?" he asked with a sort of dulled incredulity.
"What, you was about to come or somethin'?"

"Or something," Quinn moaned.

Life exhaled.

"Want me to do it again?" he asked.

Quinn exhaled.

"I don't know what I want," she said and rolled away
from Life, her back to him. Life turned his back to her. This
was the furthest thing from the truth. She wanted Life to
go away right then. She wanted to be by herself. She
wanted to wake up by herself. She wanted to start
tomorrow alone.

Calling Life... she hesitated. She was about to admit
that it had been a mistake, but then realizing that had she
not called him she might have regretted it, she realized that
calling Life had been the right thing to do, it just hadn't
turned out right. She had gotten her sex, but she hadn't
gotten any satisfaction out of it. It didn't make sense. If sex
was supposed to be for nothing else, it was supposed to be
for satisfaction. What sense did it make to have sex if you
weren't satisfied? That was like sleeping for ten hours and
waking up tired.

Quinn turned around and grabbed Life by the balls. Oh
well, she thought to herself, no sense going to sleep if she
wasn't satisfied.

She watched Life over a cup of coffee the next morning
as he dressed. She had missed him a little since they had

broken up over a month ago. They'd been together for a year and, though she believed the relationship to be doomed from almost the beginning, she had hung on to a glimmer of hope up until the month before. By then, she couldn't take it any more. She had imagined, in the beginning, that with a name like Life he'd be an experience that included a little bit of everything. She was surprised that he was so full of hard knocks. But as he slipped his shirt on, all she was thinking about was how she felt sometimes in his arms. How she liked the way that he smelled. How he rolled up his socks and put them in his boots whenever he was about to make love to her. How they did 'things' with each other that she had never really done before. 'Things' she thought she might never do and sure as hell thought she would never do again. How they did so many 'things' that she didn't know if there were 'things' left to do. That was why Carmen's offer had intrigued her so. That was something left to do. She had wanted to tell Life. To suggest it to him. But the image of Life bouncing Carmen's big ass off his stomach was way too violent for her, so she left it alone.

Life kissed her on his way out the door, which was nice, and the flood of pleasant memories that came in like clean water in a washing machine sloshed around in Quinn's mind before being met by their dirty laundry. Life had cheated on her. He pushed her around. He had always seemed jealous of her and competitive. Worst of all, he didn't seem to understand why she wasn't satisfied. How she could want more when she already had a job, occasional singing gigs and him.

"It's like you're being disrespectful to God," he would say when she spoke on what she wanted for herself. "You should be thankful for what you have."

"I am thankful," she would counter. "But I want even more to be thankful about."

He would shake his head and she would shake hers and that's where they would end the conversation. Maybe he would kiss her, eager for some pussy, or maybe she would get up and walk over to the stereo, put on the headphones, sit on the floor and turn on some Sarah Vaughn. In any event, their impasse would have been reached and anything that happened for the rest of the night would be done for the satisfaction of one or the other, never both.

Quinn twisted her lips into a closed scowl. This morning hadn't ended like that though. Thank God, she moaned to herself and wished that Life had been around to hear her. Rather, she wished that God had been around to hear her. Sometimes it seemed to her that either He wasn't listening, or He was listening and laughing with all the angels about how ridiculous and pathetic she was. He couldn't have been taking her seriously. If He were, she'd already be a star.

Quinn's mother Maxine had had this old Roberta Flack album, *Chapter 2*. The first song on it was this song called 'Reverend Lee'. On it, the devil's daughter tempted a very upright reverend, seducing him into seducing her. Quinn would play that record over and over again when she had discovered it at age fourteen, sometimes imagining herself the devil's daughter and Reverend Lee to be a man that looked somewhat like Levarr Burton from *Roots*. She had a thing for him. She liked the color of his skin, the texture of his hair, the thickness of his lips. And the way he looked in those chains...

Anyway, she knew the devil to be the epitome of evil and all, but she couldn't imagine a just God making the devil's daughter anything but an innocent. Kids rebelled. Why'd the devil's daughter necessarily have to be evil?

Quinn would sneak *Chapter 2* from its normal place of storage among the other family albums in the living room, to her room and the little portable stereo her father had bought her to play her New Edition records. And there she would lay, listening to Reverend Lee, imagining Reverend Levarr and touching herself in such a way she imagined that if a man was good for nothing else, he should at least be able relieve her of this burden. She'd mouth the words, her enjoyment building at the climax of the song. One day her mother walked in.

"Reverend Lee!" Quinn was screaming, her eyes closed, her hand in her panties. *"Come and do it to me! Reverend Lee..."*

"Come and do what to you?" Maxine deadpanned. Quinn bounced into a sitting position, opening her eyes and yanking her hand out of her panties.

"Help me sing the rest of this song," she said off-handedly.

"That's all you want help with?" Maxine asked, motioning with her head and her eyes towards her daughter's hand, panties, and then the combination of the two together.

"I was just..." Quinn began. "You know..."

"Doin' it to Reverend Lee?" Maxine asked, raised an eyebrow.

Quinn, unable to think of anything else to do, laughed. Maxine joined her. Quinn was relieved beyond words.

"Work on the singing," Maxine said, becoming serious as she turned from her daughter and started out the bedroom door. "Don't work on finding a real-life Reverend Lee."

Work on the singing, Quinn thought, once her mother had left the room. That suggestion had been too much like encouragement. Maxine hadn't been too big on encouragement when Quinn was younger. Her thing was laws and law enforcement. She handled both. Quinn's father, Greg, was big on encouragement. So much so, though, that Quinn never knew when to trust him. Everything she did couldn't be "Just wonderful, baby." Of course, as Quinn got older, Maxine became her biggest fan and Greg, the world's biggest cynic.

Quinn did work on the singing, though, forming a band not long after getting caught with her pants down. It wasn't really a band. It was just four girls who thought they could sing and one who played the drums. The four would all meet up over the drum playing girl's house and write songs while the drum playing girl played the same rhythm over and over again, telling them it was something she had just come up with to match whatever song had just been written. Finally, after the 200th variation of 'So-So Fine', Quinn's one-day-to-be smash hit, she quit the band. She was tired of the other girls. None of them worked as hard as she did and they all expected to be bigger stars than she was gonna be. Besides, they were all jealous of her. She could tell. She had been the first one to make rocking puffy green socks and aerobic sneakers a look. Now the look was a sort of unofficial group thing. A thing that the other girls in the group didn't really give her credit for either. And if there was one thing that those girls and everybody else needed to learn and understand about Quinn, it was that she would never stand for a lack of appreciation.

So Quinn was on her own again. It seemed like she was always on her own. Or with somebody, wishing she was on her own. This is what she was thinking about as the door closed behind Life. She pictured him, walking down the stairs of her apartment, wondering where he stood. If he were lucky, he would stand on his feet. She knew he wanted her back. But there was no coming back. There were only midnight rendezvous and the satisfaction of occasional needs until, soon, even those needs would be getting filled elsewhere. She thought of the pretty-eyed boy and smiled. He would do, she thought. He would do.

The only thing Quinn had ever hated about starting a new relationship was the dishonesty of it all. Nobody could ever say exactly what they wanted or meant. It was as if they had to watch a stranger take over their bodies and say things that they would never say simply not to terrify away the person sitting across the table from them. The pretty-eyed boy seemed so innocent. How long would it be before she told him that she was divorced? Or how many dicks she had sucked? Or how many abortions she had had? Or that thing she had done in college that time with the two boys? Or that thing she had done a couple of years before the boy and the other girl? Or her year as a practising lesbian? How much of this would sicken him? Repulse him? Turn him off? Turn him away? She knew that even if he had done any or all of the same, that sort of behavior from her would be totally unacceptable. Men, it seemed, wanted to believe themselves more experienced sexually than any woman they could see themselves being serious about. That pretty, innocent-eyed boy with his — what — maybe twenty or thirty experiences, would be no match for her expertise and she could already picture herself at an East Village soul food restaurant somewhere, lying like the truth had gone out of style.

"I've only had two serious boyfriends," she'd say in her

cute-as-a-pixie voice, almost blushing under the weight of her assumed innocence. She'd watch him swell like a man, feeling good about himself and the prospect of conquering very infrequently tilled soil.

"And we didn't do too much either," she'd continue and he'd swell some more, this time to the point where it seemed like he might burst.

"I mean, I had to quit the second guy when he suggested that I... you know," and she'd motion with her eyes towards her groin. "Go down below," she'd whisper.

It would be at this point that she could almost hear his hard-on tapping the bottom of the table. Then would start the process. The kiss on the first night, nothing more than a brushing of the lips. A little bit of tongue on the next date, a moan that seemed to escape and embarrass her, forcing her to flee because it seemed that she was getting too caught up in the moment. He might get to fondle a tittie or two on the third date. His dick would be rock hard, certainly. She'd let him get to the point where he was lifting her shirt and pulling back her bra to suck it when she'd have to stop him. This always killed Quinn. Knowing how much she liked her titties sucked. He'd get to suck them on the next night and if he did a good job, I mean, a really good job, he might get a little pussy that night too. If not, it might take him another couple of nights.

She remembered how she had got lucky with Life. Well, for the time being. Life was just getting out of jail and wasn't looking for a good girl. This was good because Quinn, at that moment, wasn't looking for a man. It was right after her lesbian thing. She still liked niggas though. This much she could admit to herself. Still, re-crossing the gender line would require just the right specimen. He'd have to be big, muscular, black, and manly. So when Life walked into her set that night wearing a twisted black Yankee fitted cap with the 'NY' letters blackened in, a black Nike hooded sweatshirt and a pair of olive colored army fatigues and black Timberlands, Quinn knew she'd found her specimen. He just stood there in the back of the club, neither looking at the band nor looking away, focused instead it seemed, on himself, his eyes merely recording the atmosphere.

Quinn liked him from the start, from the distance. The fact that he was dressed the way he was dressed in a midtown club populated by suits and ties, whites and gays, niggas and their white girlfriends, made him sexy as hell by comparison. She knew he hadn't come to listen to the jazz she was singing or the band that was playing and, sure enough, as soon as they had taken a break, the drummer sought him out and they walked outside the club and disappeared. The drummer returned five minutes later. Life did not.

"Who was that?" Quinn whispered to the drummer as he took his place on the stand.

"That was my man," the drummer said.

"What's he got?" Quinn asked.

"What do you need?" the drummer said.

"Some dick," Quinn said, then turned a hue darker, blushing under her brown skin.

"He's got that too," the drummer said, sounding just a

little too confident.

"You fucked him?" Quinn asked.

"I wish," the drummer said, flashing just a glimpse of the secret self he kept buried from his fellow band mates.

"So he's straight?"

"He won't let me suck his dick," the drummer lamented.

"You asked?" Quinn couldn't believe it.

"Girl, you know I did," the drummer chuckled.

Quinn started to make a teasing homo joke but quickly remembered that she herself was just coming out of a year-long lesbian relationship and yielded. The drummer would have been all over her if she hadn't.

"Can you get him back here?" she asked, referring to Life.

"Not tonight," the drummer said. "He never delivers to the same place twice in one night. He thinks it might be a set-up or something."

"When's the next time he'll come?"

"Tomorrow."

So there Quinn was the following night, her tightest top making her titties rise like baking bread, an African wrap that she had bought at a downtown Brooklyn boutique surrounding her hips, her hair tightly cornrowed, her lips in a nervous snarl. It was before the set and she was in the bathroom, feeling at the point of nausea. Why was she so nervous? This guy Life was just a guy. There had been many before, there would be many after. It didn't help that the drummer still hadn't arrived. The sax player was the only one who had been on time to rehearse. The bass player had come in with a white girl that he had strategically placed near the back of the restaurant, near the door. The trumpet player's case of herpes simplex one had flared up leaving a hideous mucus-colored fever blister bulging from the right side of his top lip. And the piano player had gotten a studio gig paying about five times as much as he would have earned if he had played tonight, and had to be replaced at the last minute by that asshole: Phil Flarn.

"Let's get it on, bay-bee," Phil Flarn had come in chanting, bopping his head like the strains of the song he was miming was playing in his head despite the fact that he wasn't wearing headphones. He was dressed wrong, which, of course, was no surprise. He was wearing shorts, for crissakes. Topped by a white T-shirt under a cheap imitation Latrell Sprewell Knicks jersey and Allen Iverson orange and white Reebok sneakers.

Phil sat down at the piano and began cracking his knuckles.

"What?" he asked under the glare of Quinn's watchful eye.

Quinn couldn't say anything. She could only shake her head. So she did. Suddenly, she felt sick. She ran towards the back of the stage, towards the bathroom.

"My clothes are in the cleaners," Phil shouted behind her. "I'm having them delivered."

Quinn closed the door. Nothing could ever go totally right. It wasn't as if she hadn't spent the entire night before figuring on how she'd seduce this guy Life. It wasn't as if she hadn't gone over it a thousand times in her mind. And in each replay, the drummer was on time, the sax player had a black girlfriend, the trumpet player had genital herpes, and the piano player was not that asshole: Phil Flarn.

Shaun had called Quinn one night about a year before when Alanda just happened to be over.

"What you doing?" Shaun asked on his cell phone.

"Nothing," Quinn said. "Alanda's here. We're just chilling. About to smoke."

"I wanna bring my man by," Shaun had said. "He plays piano. He just started in my band. He smokes."

"Alright," Quinn said, trying to sound as if she hadn't heard what she had heard or knew what she knew. What she knew was Phil Flarn, by reputation, of course. Alanda and Shaun had a thing going and since Phil had just started in the band, Shaun was still in the process of taking Phil around and introducing him to the circuit.

Phil had been a hip-hop pianist, going into the studio with rappers and other assorted low-lives and playing chords and riffs while they rhymed about murder, forced abortions and genocide. Well, at least that's how the jazz community saw it. And that's how some had seen Phil, initially. Phil was nice, Quinn had heard. He had been given the stamp of approval by Shaun himself, who had one of the most discriminating ears for music she had ever known. And now he was coming to her house. Alanda had already seen him. She said he was sorta cute, sorta tall, a little goofy, but certainly Quinn's type. Quinn couldn't wait. Then they came, Shaun and Phil.

Phil seemed out of place from the beginning, sitting in

a far chair when everybody else had made himself or herself comfortable on the sofa. And there he sat, in a big floppy fisherman's hat, wordless.

"Would you like something to drink, Phil?" Quinn thought she was breaking the ice by asking.

"What do you got?" Phil asked.

"Beer, water, orange juice, Coke, milk."

"Nah, I don't want any of that," Phil said flatly. "Got any bourbon?"

As the night progressed, Quinn felt herself wavering. She felt simultaneously attracted and repulsed by Phil. He was either relentlessly arrogant or painfully unassuming. He was either devilishly handsome or starkly plain. He was either being totally charming or a complete jerk. Quinn couldn't call it. This was what was keeping her on the fence. She didn't know what to think of him yet. Then it happened. Out of nowhere, Phil Flarn got up and walked towards her stereo.

"What's this?" he asked, holding up a CD for all to see. It was *Dummy* by Portishead. Quinn's lesbian 'thing' had turned her on to it.

"That?" Quinn asked a little nervously. "That's something you'd have to have really open sensibilities to appreciate."

"Put it on," Phil Flarn demanded.

Quinn shook her head.

"I don't think you're ready for it," she said. When Phil Flarn flashed a wide, wickedly toothy grin, Quinn fell off the fence. This guy was an asshole.

"Put it on," Phil Flarn demanded again. "I may not

have any class…" he mocked wiping his nose with the back of his shirtsleeve, "…but I'll try not to laugh out loud at this shit."

Quinn shook her head.

"No, really that's okay," she said.

"C'mon, play it," Phil Flarn continued. Then he began chanting:

"We want Portishead!"

"We want Portishead!"

"We want Portishead!"

"We want Portishead!"

"Shaun, who did you bring over here?" Quinn asked, incredulous.

"Phil," Shaun interrupted, embarrassed.

Phil Flarn turned towards Shaun, seemed to go into a self-induced trance, then sat back down in the chair away from everybody else.

"See, my shit's here," Phil Flarn was saying to Quinn now. She had come out of the bathroom and he had already changed. He looked quite sharp, actually. He was wearing a black shirt over black slacks and black shoes. There was nothing fancy to his attire, but at least everything was professional. A fleeting thought concerning Phil Flarn passed through Quinn's mind as her eyes lit up seeing the drummer come through the door; she had never actually heard the asshole play.

"Aw man, homo… I mean homie," Phil Flarn laughingly greeted the drummer.

"Flarn, you know you want a piece of this," the drummer mocked.

"Not unless I get to be on top," Phil Flarn mocked in return.

"Ill," Quinn said, asserting herself as a member of the conversation.

Phil and the drummer both laughed.

"What time's my boyfriend getting here?" Quinn asked the drummer.

"I told him to come after the first set. At about nine," the drummer said.

Quinn nodded unevenly, uncomfortably.

"Quinn, you got a man?" Phil Flarn asked in a tone that seemed just inside sincerity.

Quinn shook her head.

"Nah, but I'm about to get one," she said firmly. Phil Flarn raised both eyebrows then went and took a seat behind the piano. The drummer sat down next. Quinn was left standing alone at the center of the stage. She looked at the clock on the wall to her right. It read seven-thirty. The show was about to start.

Only the drummer wasn't surprised by the number of black faces in the crowd seated at tables behind plates of food and glasses of wine and champagne. He had taken the precaution of inviting a number of friends. With a quick glance through, Quinn spotted several faces she knew, among them Shaun, who she was more shocked to see than Santa Claus.

Phil Flarn was playing. The word was that Phil Flarn had just left Shaun's band one day without as much as an excuse and there was beef. But as Quinn's eyes traveled from Shaun in front of her to Phil Flarn behind her, they seemed to acknowledge each other and the acknowledgement seemed to be friendly. Okay then, Quinn thought to herself, an hour and a half more of this shit and I get to meet my man.

There was something different about the sound of the music they were making that night. Quinn noticed it almost from the start. It sounded crisper, as if every note of one particular instrument was both dictating and keeping the pace of all the other music being played. As she sang song after song she listened, going through her head about the source of the change. Quinn started to glance quickly around at the band whenever a note she sang provided her with the opportunity to turn her head. The drummer was doing what he had done the night before, with the exception of the fact that he was working harder at it. Beads of sweat on his forehead had replaced the prior night's effortless taps. The trumpet player was working the shit out of his cold sore. He seemed to have bitten it off because there was blood on his mouthpiece and a round, pink, bleeding circle on his lip where it had been. The sax player was making lascivious eye contact with a pretty black girl in the front row while his white girlfriend fumed in the back. Phil Flarn simply played.

It's Phil Flarn, it occurred to Quinn as she listened again, this time simply for him.

Phil Flarn wasn't the stumbling type. Well, at least he wasn't right then. His keystrokes were like the sound of cold, crisp lettuce being torn apart. Each note was sharp, intended to be its own Alpha and Omega and no two sounds ran together even if he was striking more than one key at a time. He wasn't even looking at his piano. He was talking, audibly, to Shaun out in the audience. Quinn could hear him. She was sure that Shaun couldn't hear, much less anybody else in the audience, but he must have believed that Shaun could read his lips because he sure as hell kept on talking. Quinn was amazed.

"I'm trying to get some pussy, dawg," she heard him say, and almost missed a note of her own wondering who would fuck this lunatic.

Then Life walked in. This time, he was wearing a form-fitting light gray sweater and a pair of deep blue jeans and blue Nike jogging sneakers. Everybody seemed to notice him. Even Phil Flarn who Quinn heard ask rhetorically, "That your man?"

He sat down in the only available seat. It was near the stage. It was only eight-forty-five and for the next fifteen minutes, Quinn had to sing looking all around the club, as if she hadn't even noticed the beautiful stranger sitting at her feet. When nine o'clock came, she allowed herself to look at him. He was already looking at her. She smiled a sort of, "How's it going?" smile as if she had no idea who he was or why he was there. Then the drummer hopped off the stage and greeted him.

"Sup Life?" the drummer asked, becoming immediately butch.

"Sup Trent?" Life asked in return as the other members of the band stood, stretched and began to seek out members of the audience whom they knew. Phil Flarn made a beeline for Shaun. Quinn sort of lilted from the stage, seeming not to know what to do with herself but settling conveniently near Life and the drummer.

"Oh," the drummer said, giggling and becoming almost girly for just a second. "Life this is Quinn. Quinn this is Life."

"How do you do?" he asked.

How do you do? she was thinking. How long had it been since a man had actually asked her how she did?

"I do alright," she said with a slow smile and when it was returned the drummer began to feel that he would soon no longer be necessary so it would be best to settle that little bit of business he had pending with Life.

"You wanna go outside to do what we gotta do?" the drummer asked and Life, a businessman first, looked away from Quinn's titties long enough to look at the drummer and nod.

"Outside?" Phil Flarn asked excitedly from across the room. "Who's going outside?"

The drummer laughed.

"You can come Phil," the drummer said. "I know how you get down."

"Damn right," Phil Flarn said as he began walking towards the group of Life, the drummer and Quinn, leaving Shaun standing alone. As soon as Phil Flarn reached the group, they were turning, headed towards the front door. They exited quietly. Life frowned at a busy 8th Avenue.

"Let's go around the corner," he ordered in the form of a suggestion. Everybody followed his lead. They found a sleeping building entrance somewhere on 50th Street.

"Ex for you Trent?" Life asked the drummer.

The drummer nodded excitedly. He pulled out of his front pocket a twenty-dollar bill and a five and handed it to Life. Life reached into the fifth pocket of his jeans, pulled out then handed the drummer the little off-white pill in a small, clear plastic bag.

"Whadda you want?" Life asked Phil Flarn flatly.

"Whadda you got?" Phil Flarn asked Life just as flatly.

"Whatever you want," Life said. "Trust me."

Phil Flarn looked thoughtful.

"Just gimme a twenty of some weed," Phil Flarn said finally.

"Whatchu want, brown or green?" Life asked.

"Brown," Phil Flarn said. Life reached his back pocket where the imprint of a wallet had seemed evident and pulled out a soft leather pouch that covered an assortment of bagged herbs. He selected a bag containing brown herb and handed it to Phil Flarn as Flarn produced a twenty.

"Damn!" Phil Flarn said upon receiving the weed. "Now I gotta go to the store and get a Dutch."

"Not a problem," Life said. He bent over and reached down, pulling up his pants leg.

"What'd you want?" Life asked, still bent over. "A Dutch?"

"Yeah," Phil Flarn said. When Life was standing erect again, a Dutch Master cigar was in his hand.

"How much?" Phil Flarn asked.

"Seventy-five cents," Life said. Phil Flarn nodded.

"That's the same as the store," he said.

Life shrugged.

"I do it like a service, you know?" he said. Phil Flarn

nodded. Life turned to Quinn.

"You want anything?" he asked.

Quinn shook her head at first, then thinking better of it added, "I'll get what I want from you later, if you're lucky."

"Ooooh…" went the chorus moaned by Phil Flarn and the drummer simultaneously.

"So this is what you do?" Quinn asked Life as Phil Flarn used a key to cut open the cigar and empty its contents of tobacco.

"A little of it," Life said with a slight shrug. "I'm trying to get into the music industry too. I got these kids I manage. They rhyme. They're nice as shit."

"Where they from?" Phil Flarn asked, now beginning to crumble the bagged herbs into the emptied cigar casing.

"White Plains," Life said.

"Ooh," Phil Flarn moaned. "Non-New York City niggas. I'm always down with non-New York City niggas."

"That's cause you a non-New York City nigga," the drummer mocked. "New London mothafucka."

"Don't knock 'The Sixth Borough'," Phil Flarn warned. "The greatest piano player you'll ever hear live came outta New London, New York."

"Who's the greatest piano player he'll ever hear live?" Quinn asked innocently.

Phil Flarn lit the blunt, took a long drag, then deadpanned Quinn.

"Oh…" she said, laughing a little. "You really think you're that good?"

Phil Flarn nodded vigorously.

"I mean," he began, speaking through the smoke in his

lungs, "I don't think I'm the greatest ever. Monk was the greatest ever. But I'm second."

"All-time?" the drummer asked in a sort of mocking incredulous tone.

Phil Flarn nodded and exhaled a hazy breath of smoke.

"What about Duke Ellington?" Quinn asked.

"Bum," Phil Flarn said quickly.

"McCoy Tyner?" the drummer asked.

"Bum."

"Count Basie?" Quinn asked.

"Bum."

"Herbie Hancock?" the drummer asked.

"So overrated," Phil Flarn said with a dismissive shake of his head.

"Bud Powell?" Life asked.

Phil Flarn raised an impressed eyebrow.

"Nice," he began, "but I'll still burn him."

"You are good, Phil," Quinn said as the memory of him playing earlier was occurring to her.

"And you are smart," Phil Flarn said before taking another long drag on his blunt. After he inhaled he hummed, raised his eyebrows, and pushed the burning marijuana in the general direction of everybody, making an offer. The drummer took the blunt from him. He aimed it towards his mouth then paused.

"You don't mind smoking with somebody that sucks dick?" he mocked as Phil Flarn was exhaling, forgetting then shrugging off the fact that he had just 'outted' himself to Life.

"Nah, you saw me offer it to Quinn, didn't you?" Phil

Flarn said without missing a beat.

Life laughed. Quinn didn't.

"How do you know I suck dick?" Quinn asked, a little uncomfortably.

"I don't," Phil Flarn said evenly. "I'm just considering the alternatives."

"Ooooh," the drummer moaned, before finally taking a long inhale of the blunt. Being the only person other than Quinn that knew that she was just coming out of a year-long lesbian relationship, the drummer was now potentially dangerous. Quinn became a little more nervous. It wasn't that she didn't want Life to think she was a freak. It was just that she didn't want him to think that she was any particular kind of freak. Men expected different things from different kinds of freaks.

"You a pussy eater?" Phil Flarn asked of Life causing all eyes to turn to him. The drummer's inhale was interrupted by an unexpected laughing cough.

"It depends," Life said after a moment.

"On what?" Quinn asked so quickly that it surprised everybody.

"The girl," Life said simply. All seemed reassured.

"Good," Phil Flarn said. "We'll balance out on the blunt with these two cocksuckers."

"Ill," Quinn moaned as Life and the drummer laughed.

"Phil, I think you sucked a little dick before," the drummer teased.

"Nah nigga," Phil Flarn said, shaking his head in correction. "If I was gonna suck a dick, it'd be a big one. I wouldn't suck a little dick. I don't be fuckin' around."

Life was shaking his head and chuckling. Quinn was only shaking her head. The drummer had dropped to his knees in tears. He passed the blunt up to Quinn. She took a deep inhale. The drummer returned to his feet.

The camaraderie of the weed smokers either erased all politics or enhanced them. And as those four stood there on 50th Street off 8th Avenue becoming friends for life, the moment they shared was more honest than if they'd all been sipping truth serum. And it wasn't so much that the truth was being told. It was just so heavily implied. Phil Flarn and the drummer were no dummies. Each could tell that if either or both Quinn and Life played their cards right, they'd be together and naked soon. The drummer himself was exposed without the wanton faggot role he assumed for the benefit of most. He was a talented drummer. He was, in fact, one of the best in New York. And he was a pretty smart dude. Phil Flarn was exposed, perhaps the most easily. All could see through his front of arrogance to his core of insecurities. He was really a good piano player and he had to know it somewhere deep within his core. Still, it seemed as if he needed to be continually convinced and like Muhammad Ali screaming, "I am The Greatest", Phil Flarn was always eager to tear down any other piano player in the entire history of the instrument if it would better champion a case for himself.

"I'm nice as shit on the keys," Phil Flarn said, taking the last drag from the dying blunt.

"You are," the drummer said, nodding deadpan.

"And I'ma show y'all," Phil Flarn continued. He turned to Quinn. "What's that song you got, girl?"

Quinn looked confused and then a little afraid.

"You know what song I'm talking about," Phil Flarn continued, nudging Quinn with his elbow.

Quinn frowned, squinted and shook her head.

" 'Love Supreme' or 'Love Hangover' or 'Sweetest Taboo' or 'How Do U Want It' or something like that?" Phil Flarn continued.

" 'Lover Man'," the drummer toned in.

" 'Lover Man'," Phil Flarn said nodding. "That's what we're gonna do when we go back inside, 'Lover Man'."

Quinn looked nervously at Life who looked at her blank-eyed. She didn't know what she was expecting to find in his eyes. He didn't know the significance of that song to her. She didn't even know how that asshole: Phil Flarn had heard about it. Now he was about to call her out on it, not only in front of an audience of strangers, but in front of this boy Life that she just might start to develop a thing for. That asshole: Phil Flarn.

The four walked in silence back towards 8th Avenue and the entrance of the club. When they walked in the door they were greeted by a sarcastic applause that let them know that they had overstayed their break from the first set. Life returned to his seat near the back. The drummer led the crusade back toward the stage, followed by Quinn and Phil Flarn, who walked with his head bowed and both middle fingers extended upwards, eliciting even more applause.

"That's okay," Phil Flarn mocked into the mic when he returned to the stage. "We're gonna do a song now that's gonna shut all that shit up." He looked around at the band.

"Everybody follow me," he said to the drummer, trumpet player and sax. He then asked Quinn for the key. She gave it to him. And he began to play.

Life's dick was so deep inside Quinn's throat that she wondered absently if he could tell how hungry she was. It had been so long. She wanted so badly to suck his dick. Possibly even more than she wanted to fuck him. In the year that she had been with that girl, they'd done a lot of things. They owned a lot of mechanisms that made for pretty good simulated intercourse with a man, whenever that sensation was needed. But there had been nothing that could match the real-life sensation of a large, warm, pulsing penis resting along the top of her tongue. This is what I miss, Quinn thought, as she began sliding her head back and forth, jabbing his stomach with her forehead. He was beginning to tense and she could feel it. Suddenly, she didn't want him to come. It had been over a year. She decided to fuck him, if only to see if she remembered the workings of a man correctly. To see if she remembered how different it was from when her ex-girlfriend would go and get the supplies. Without a word, Quinn turned and faced the opposite direction, her hands and knees on the floor underneath her.

She had to fuck him after singing to him, she thought as she descended the stage earlier that evening. Everything about 'Lover Man' had been everything about him. Quinn had never heard music like the sounds coming from the band on that song and it was as if even her voice wasn't her own. She recognized the words; she had sung them enough before in the past, but the way that they escaped from her throat was so very different. And it was as if, for once, Phil Flarn wasn't such an asshole. It was as if he was in on it. The way he played... God must have been playing through him.

"Fuck y'all," Phil Flarn said into the microphone after the song was over. "Don't applaud. Y'all applauded when we walked in the door late. Now y'all gotta boo."

So the audience booed. And it was the loudest longest boo that anyone there could ever remember hearing.

The band played out the rest of the set and Quinn sang the songs as they came, one by one, but it was really like a post-orgasmic chat. The audience had already cum. When the last of the songs was over, Phil Flarn jumped to his feet, looked at his pager and screamed, "Aw shit!" then ran out of the club dodging the traffic on 8th Avenue before disappearing down into a subway entrance.

Quinn thanked the audience for all the band members. They applauded like their palms itched.

"That was crazy," Shaun said, the first to rush up to Quinn once the show was over. "Who wrote that song?"

"I did," Quinn said simply. Then more people came, touching and just wanting to be next to her. She warmed with each touch and returned kind words like a tennis player returning serve. She thanked and acknowledged, bowing her head humbly before the overflow of compliments searching, checking and rechecking all the while to make sure that Life had gone nowhere. He stayed where he was, waiting patiently.

"Damn, girl," Joyce began, emerging out of nowhere.

"You murdered that song."

"Thank you," Quinn said, squinting with surprise at seeing her friend, before leaning over and kissing her just to the right of Joyce's full pink lips.

"Who was that piano player?" Joyce asked a little too innocently.

Quinn became panicked.

"No," she said. "That's Phil Flarn. He's an asshole. You don't wanna mess with him. He's crazy."

Joyce nodded and all, looking as if she might be taking her friend's words of advice to heart, but there was a bit of intrigue lingering in her eyes. Quinn could tell.

Quinn remembered when Joyce had first come on the scene. Joyce was a singer too. She had a damn good voice too. It was kind of scary because it was undisciplined but what it lacked in training it made up for in raw, naked appeal. Joyce had come to New York from Atlanta with her daughter. This was after going to college of all things and singing everywhere from the church to the college choir to doing back-up studio work with R&B and hip-hop groups. Now she was into jazz. And jazz was into her. Quinn would have never admitted it to herself, but she did feel a little intimidated by Joyce. They were both tall women and what Quinn lacked in hips, Joyce more than made up for. Plus, Joyce's looks matched her voice; wild and raw, light-skinned and crazy-eyed with angular features that seemed to have been sculptured by a madman. And her personality was tempered with the most savagely easygoing indifference. Like anything she wanted, she could have. Quinn just hoped for her sake that she didn't want Phil Flarn.

"Hmm," Joyce said, after seemingly pondering Quinn's last thought in her own mind. "Hmm," she said again, as if she was making sure that Quinn had heard her the first time.

Quinn was being kissed again before she remembered that she and Joyce weren't alone. The pats on the back were beating her down. She decided to start to make her way over to Life.

"You wanna go somewhere and grab a drink or something?" she asked when she reached his table, the eyes of the club heavy upon them both.

"Sure," he said simply.

"Let me grab my coat," Quinn said, and with that headed back through the hail of back-pats towards the stage area where her coat rested on a hook hanging behind the drum set. The drummer shot her a knowing wink. She winked back. Two hours later, Life was sliding inside her from behind.

Quinn moaned on the entry, enjoying the sensation of a real, live human cock like it was the first bite of food after Ramadan. Life seemed to realize what Quinn had been missing and, as an act of mercy/torture, he gave it to her slow, long and hard. Quinn rocked with his movements, her tongue tasting the bottom of her front teeth, her back arching with each slow thrust, her elbows becoming weak as the intruder tapped her somewhere around her belly button.

"Ugh," she moaned, causing him to miss a beat, his stroke becoming violent with the accident, causing her to

moan again, this time louder, causing his stroke to go
further awry until the whole thing deteriorated and they
were fucking. With each stroke came a moan and with each
moan came a stroke until she became an instrument and he
was banging her trying to get the perfect sound. When it
came, so did he.

They were facing each other now. Her, sitting upright
on the sofa. Him, sitting Indian-style on the floor. Both
were breathing hard. Quinn looked down at herself. Her
breasts seemed huge. Her nipples were like projectiles
shooting from the head of a rocket ship. She plucked one,
squeezing it between her thumb and forefinger. It
reminded her of how much work remained to be done.

"What's on your mind?" Life asked, the sight of
Quinn's tittie-touch not lost on him.

"I don't remember your answer," Quinn said evenly.

"To what?" Life asked, honestly perplexed.

"To Phil Flarn's question."

"Which one?"

"You a pussy eater?" Quinn asked.

Life smiled.

"Depends on the woman," he said, climbing to his
knees and beginning to crawl between Quinn's legs. She
pulled them back, using her hands to hold her thighs high.
He zeroed right in.

Now it was over.

The beginning of a relationship is always good, Quinn
reminded herself. That's why you get in it. That wasn't
true. Some of her best relationships had started off bad.
She remembered when she had been singing in a band

started by this guy named Cedric. Cedric was a drummer. Cedric was a straight drummer. He worked with Shaun sometimes and his band was up and coming. Cedric had a temper. When things didn't go right, it was everybody else's fault. But Cedric was a damn good drummer and Quinn was always drawn to the exceptional, even if it was for only one exception.

When they started having sex, Cedric had a girlfriend and Quinn felt bad about it. Well, she didn't actually feel bad. She wouldn't have been doing it if she felt that bad. What she felt was incomplete. There was something wrong. There was only one thing wrong. But there was something wrong. When the girlfriend was gone, things still didn't feel right. There was something else wrong. Something was always wrong. But the problem seemed so easy to fix, the solution so within reach, that they'd keep at it. They'd eliminate a named problem, only to find a new one ready to step in almost immediately. They got married anyway. That didn't help. And the funny thing is, neither ever found out what the problem was.

Now she was expected to be a new woman again for that asshole: Phil Flarn's friend, the pretty-eyed boy. As if he was gonna even make half an attempt to be a new man. That was the worst part about being a woman, Quinn had always felt. A man was respected more the more he did. A woman was respected less. So judging from her first real assessment of this pretty-eyed boy, she could either be painfully close to virginity, or ready to become a complete freak. Which essentially meant the same thing.

But she was thinking about it too hard, she knew. She

was too worried about it. Nothing good ever happened when you worried. There were a million special boys, some with pretty eyes, some without. If she thought about this boy too hard, he'd be a mess. He'd be unemployed with twelve kids, thirteen baby mothers, living with his mother and not paying rent. He'd have crabs, chronic halitosis, urine-tinged body odor and court appearances into the next decade. Or she could just not like his dick.

The phone rang.

No way, she thought.

"Hello?" she answered.

"Quinn," he said.

"Yes?" she asked.

"This is Caesar. Caesar Brown. I was with Phil Flarn the other night at that party…?"

C aesar was from New London, New York. It was a small town north of the city. It felt like a small town. Businesses in the town were named after it. When he was a kid, Caesar would notice things on his trips to the city, like the fact that there was no New York High School. But there was a New London High. So he got the idea that life was good. There wasn't too much to have to keep up with here in his small town of New London. He could set his mind loose on other things. But every now and again he would come to hang out with Phil Flarn. He'd grown up with Phil. He loved Phil. Phil was a funny dude. He was always right in the middle of something. Right then, it was Joyce. Caesar liked Joyce and Phil together. It was the happiest middle he'd seen Phil in, in a while.

Anyway, it was Phil and Joyce who had invited him to that party. Caesar liked hanging out with the two of them. They were like a sit-com.

Caesar had met up with Phil at Phil's place in Brooklyn. They went straight to the party. Joyce was late, taking the baby to her mother's place. She was catching a cab from uptown. Anyway, being a part-time DJ, Caesar hated the music being played in the joint almost as much as he hated the joint itself. The party was in a basement. It was dark. Marijuana smoke was heavy in the air and there seemed to be a genuine feeling of animosity between the sexes. Caesar didn't really like the atmosphere. The best chance to get some pussy he'd always figured was at a well-lit club where everybody was dancing, having fun and drinking. Caesar didn't smoke weed, but he knew it made you paranoid. He couldn't imagine sexing a paranoid chick. He'd want one drunk, happy and trusting. He wanted himself that way too. That's why the well-lit club had always been best for him. People knew what they were getting into.

But there he was, at Phil's side, looking at the taa-taas on that girl across the room and through the darkness. He didn't know what it was about her, other than her taa-taas that caught his attention. But his eyes were traveling from them to her face, back and forth, back and forth. Then it turned out that Phil knew her.

He was glad that she seemed cool. Caesar wasn't too keen on the jazz scene. He liked the music and all, he just didn't like the smoke-filled rooms. He imagined the girl with the taa-taas to be a wild woman just by association. She was in Phil's circle. But she seemed cool. And of course, the taa-taas… So he got her number from Phil who got it from Joyce and he called her. He was on his way to see her now.

"Why didn't you say anything about him that day?" Carmen asked, seeming a little insulted. She was folding new white girl's baby T-shirts.

"Cause, I don't be getting all excited about meeting new niggas anymore," Quinn said quickly.

"But you're all excited now," Carmen said, nodding like she was agreeing with herself.

"I'm not all excited," Quinn said through a wide tattle-tail smile.

"What's that in your mouth touching each of your ears?" Carmen asked. "A pearl necklace?" She looked down at the new white girl's baby T-shirts and breathed a frustrated exhale. "And then to wait till the end of the day," Carmen lamented.

"Well, there's still another four hours before it happens," Quinn said, her mouth still swollen with teeth.

"Bitch," Carmen said, exasperated. "Who'd you tell? Alanda?"

"Nope," Quinn said quickly. "You're the first one I told."

Carmen's eyes shot open wide.

"I'm honored," she said, now at the point of tears.

Quinn shook her head.

"You're emotional," she said.

Carmen rushed over and patted her on the shoulder.

"No, you don't understand," she began. "We're so 'girlfriends' right now."

Quinn burst out laughing.

"This is a beautiful moment for us," Carmen breathed.

"I guess it is," Quinn said, slightly smiling.

"So what's this guy like?" Carmen asked.

Quinn frowned. She tried to explain Caesar from what she saw in him, what she had heard in his voice when they talked, and what she expected. Carmen listened intently, nodding all the way and not offering any comments or opinions until Quinn finished.

"Sounds like a freak," Carmen said definitively.

"You would say that," Quinn said, squinting at her co-worker.

"That's how Steeze was when I first met him," Carmen continued. "All nice and polite and shit. Looking in my eyes when he talked to me and acting like he was really listening to me when I talked and all. Then I get in the bed with him and he's got a squash."

"A squash," Quinn said.

Carmen nodded with her top lip upturned.

"What did he do with it?" Quinn shrieked.

Carmen deadpanned. Quinn shook her head. Carmen turned to stack some recently folded baby T-shirts on a display table behind her, her ass seeming to grow from somewhere where nothing had existed before. Quinn eyed her, amazed at the growth and wondering what that ass looked like without the snug-fitting denim that struggled so hard to contain it. When Carmen turned back around, her eyes found Quinn's. Quinn was embarrassed.

"We should just do it," Carmen offered, shocking a heat into Quinn's chest that almost made her choke. "I know you get down like that," Carmen continued, smiling.

"Ill," Quinn said, feigning sickness.

"What's 'ill', bitch," Carmen said laughing. "I know you had a girlfriend a little while ago. I heard about you."

"Who told you?" Quinn asked.

"You did," Carmen laughed. "Just now."

Quinn could only shake her head as Carmen descended into hysteria.

"You love outsmarting people, don't you?"

"It's too easy," Carmen said, shaking her head.

"Do you really wanna have sex with me?" Quinn asked, now intrigued.

Carmen looked thoughtful for a moment, then nodded unevenly.

"Why?" Quinn asked.

Again, Carmen looked thoughtful.

"You've got some big-ass titties. I guess I've always wanted to suck some big-ass titties. Might be some sorta 'back to childhood' fetish. Plus, I want my asshole eaten."

Quinn made a face like she'd just been shown a picture of her own parents doing a '69'.

"Guys always act like that's some faggot shit," Carmen continued. "Like eating a pussy is so much better than eating an ass." Quinn was thinking about what she had eaten for lunch, because if Carmen continued talking the way she was, Quinn was sure she'd see her lunch again.

"So you'd want me to eat your ass?" Quinn asked, now almost angrily.

"Hell, yeah," Carmen cheered, frowning. "That long, pink-ass tongue of yours goin' all deep inside my hole... Those big-ass titties rubbing against the back of my thighs..." She moaned. Quinn moaned a little too.

"Well, you'd have to do a little bit more than suck my titties," Quinn said, nearly shocking herself by indulging the silly girl in a fantasy that was almost certainly never going to happen.

"What do you need?" Carmen asked evenly.

Quinn was confused and alone. She was scrambling because she was late. She was supposed to meet Caesar at that Lower East Side restaurant at eight, and here it was eight-fifteen and she was still in Brooklyn. She couldn't find anything that fit right. She had picked out a pair of jeans and that was the only decision she felt comfortable about. She wanted to feel comfortable. She wanted to look comfortable. The jeans had started her on her way. But when it came to a top, she was lost. It wasn't easy to camouflage titties as big as hers. Sometimes the best solution had been to hide them in plain sight. To wear something that made them so evident that even the people that didn't wanna be rude by staring at her had no choice. She thought about how she had often fantasized about a hot summer day when she would walk out of her apartment topless and just force the world to deal with it. Just force people to look at her titties, swinging heavy under their own weight and returning to perfect form with each step. The thought turned her on a little. Made her want to touch them. She licked her index finger and thumb a little and went to pricking her right nipple with them. She closed her eyes. It felt good. Her left hand gradually began making its way down her thigh... She stopped suddenly, opening her eyes. What was she doing? What was she thinking about? The answer to both scared her. It was Carmen that she saw with her eyes closed. Carmen with her back arched, her ass high in the air, her torso bent forward to suck titties. Quinn grabbed the old, gray

Montgomery University sweatshirt she had just washed from off her bed. Caesar would just have to understand.

"You look nice," were the first words out of his mouth.

"Thanks, you do too," she said in return. She was smiling because she had expected him to say something flattering about her appearance and he had. He could stick around indefinitely if he always did what she expected.

"You been here long?" Quinn asked.

"Since eight," he said.

"I'm sorry," she said quickly after glancing at her watch and realizing that it was now a quarter past nine. "My co-worker and I got into this deep conversation and I barely had time to go home and change."

He shrugged.

"Bet you'd look good in whatever you wore," he said, his eyes and his mind on her breasts. She smiled.

"You guys ready?" the maitre d' asked.

They nodded and were shown to a table near the window. Caesar wisely offered her the row seat against the wall. She took a skull note of the move.

"So how was your day?" he asked, like he was her boyfriend already. Immediately she thought of Carmen and that preposterous offer.

"A little slow," she said sounding as if she was slightly depressed about it.

"What do you do?"

"Well, I mean, I sing," she began. "But right now I'm working at a clothing store. You know, to make ends meet."

"Which clothing store?"

"Big Niggaz."

"You work at Big Niggaz?" he asked, his eyes lighting up. Uh-oh, she thought. Another Big Nigga groupie that would probably never stop hounding her for free clothes or perhaps an introduction to Bill Pryor.

"Yep," she said, bracing herself for the onslaught.

"You know this girl named Carmen?" he asked eagerly. Quinn frowned.

"How do you know Carmen?" she asked.

"I know her boyfriend, Steeze," he said. "I'm a DJ and he works at this record company. He's been trying to get me to put a mix tape together for him."

Quinn nodded. 'Small world' she was thinking.

"Small world," she said.

"What do you think of them?" he asked.

"Of who?" Quinn asked.

"Of Steeze and Carmen," he said. "You like them?"

"As a couple?"

"As anything."

Quinn nodded.

"Yeah," she said. "I like them. I think they're cool. What do you think?"

"I think they're fuckin' nuts," he nearly roared, his voice seeming to flirt with laughter as he opened his mouth wide, exposing all his teeth. "They're crazy," he continued, shaking his head and looking away towards the other people in the restaurant. "I never seen a couple like that." He turned back to her, flashing his eyes on her. It was the first time he had done it all night and it was like the first time she remembered that he could do it. He had such pretty eyes...

"Why do you think they're so crazy?" she asked, trying to break the spell of his eyes.

"They just say whatever, you know?" he asked. "Like when I first met Steeze, he had Carmen with him and we were at this house party in the Bronx. Anyway, he starts telling me that he works at this record company and I tell him I DJ. So he's like, 'You got any of your shit on you?' and I'm like, 'Yeah. I got a tape out in the car. So he's like, 'Get it.' So I go out and get it, bring it back and he's got, like, this walkman on him and he puts the tape in it and starts playing it. So then he's like bobbin' his head like crazy, jumping and smiling to the beats and shit, then he calls his girlfriend over. He's like, 'Carmen, this is Caesar. Caesar, this is my lady Carmen. Carmen listen to this tape that this dude here just gave me.' So she puts on the headphones to the walkman and starts listening to it and shit. Then she's like, 'This is nice. This is nice, you do all this yourself?' So I nodded. Then she's like, 'You got a big dick'?"

Quinn's eyes almost popped out. Caesar was laughing.

"I know. I know!" he continued. "Then like, Steeze is like, 'Yo, she'll fuck you. She's my girl and all, but she'll fuck you. Just use a condom and shit cause we only do it raw together.' I'm like, 'What?' But he's like, 'Nah, for real. She likes the talented. She must think you're talented. That's a compliment. So now she wants to fuck you.' So while I'm standing there trying to process all this shit as opposed to just taking it all in, this guy starts trying to aggressively persuade me. He's like, 'Yo, you should fuck her, yo. She doesn't have too many titties, but look at that ass.' Then he spins her around and shows me her ass and everything, it was crazy."

"So what did you do?" Quinn asked, suddenly very conscious of her own voice.

"Nothin'," he said. "I didn't know what to do. Should I fuck her and risk the chance of pissing him off? You shouldn't fuck around with somebody's lady just because he gives you permission to. Should I not fuck her and risk the chance of pissing him off? What if he saw it as an insult that I had turned down his lady's services? I didn't know. I just wanted to be on mixtapes. So I just left it alone. I decided that I had enough problems of my own and didn't wanna get caught up in anybody else's."

Quinn was nodding and understanding but a question had been planted. Was that why Carmen had wanted to fuck her too? Because she thought Quinn was talented? Suddenly, she wanted to fuck Carmen badly.

"So you know her too?" Caesar was asking, with a look in his eye as familiar as if he was reading her mind.

"Huh?" Quinn asked nervously.

"Carmen," Caesar reiterated. "You know her too?"

"Yeah," Quinn said, her voice breaking a little. "I work with her every day."

Caesar shook his head and looked away. Quinn could tell that he was thinking about that ass. It was almost cute. She didn't find it rude, I mean, she would have thought there was something wrong with him as a man if he didn't:

1) Realize that Carmen had a big, beautifully huge ass.

2) Want it in some way, shape, or form.

The fact that he had wanted it, which she could tell by the way he admired it even from the safe distance of his thoughts, yet hadn't taken it, had proven to be a feather in his cap as far as Quinn was concerned. It was a great attribute for a man to have the ability to desire but still resist. If she got into a relationship with Caesar she'd know that he saw the other bitches of the world out there. He peeped their titties, the heavy ones and the light. He saw their hips, wide and narrow. He dug their faces, pretty and ghoulish. Their legs, sturdy or rickety. All of them, like a man was supposed to. Yet the power to decide whether or not he'd fuck them would be his. That was sexy to Quinn. Much sexier than the niggas who pretended that they weren't even attracted to other women and tried to fuck everything walking. And the men who really weren't attracted to other women and only seemed to like her. They made her feel like she was some sort of fag-hag.

The food came and there was Caesar behind a plate of blackened chicken. His hands were huge. It was a realization that caused a wrinkle in Quinn's eyebrows. He was otherwise so slight. He wasn't even six feet tall and slim. But his hands were wide with boxer's fists and he held his knife and fork like he controlled them. Two quick flashes rushed through her mind; one with those huge hands on her own breasts, the other with those same hands on Carmen's ass. Carmen... she had to get that girl out of her mind.

Quinn sipped some concoction that the restaurant passed off as an alcoholic beverage. She wasn't feeling the effects of anything. She hadn't smoked in a few days. She hadn't had any Ecstasy since her recording session with Shaun the weekend before. She didn't do coke. But she needed something right then. So she returned to the oldest high in the book. The one that came without even the stigma of illegality.

She remembered that when she was a girl, the mood of the house would change whenever there was any alcohol in it. It wasn't that her mother was an alcoholic (and this was something she told herself repeatedly throughout the course of her life) but her mother did like to drink. And her mother liked to fuck. But only after she had finished drinking. Quinn could remember hearing Al Green, always Al Green with the old stereo turned up as loud as it could go and her mother's arm, in her hand a half-full glass, swaying backwards over the arm of the sofa. She'd be singing a little with Al. Singing and laughing. Laughing mostly. Quinn would stand behind the sofa, behind her mother's arm for a while before creeping slowly around it. To where she could see a little better. There would be her father. He'd have her mother's legs pinned back to the point where it seemed the woman formed a big 'W' and he'd be pounding away, workman-like inside of her. Maxine would be laughing and singing and Greg would have an expression like a man struggling his way through the last repetition of a strenuous exercise. There'd be no joy in his face. Then he'd come. It would be an ugly sight to behold. He'd shake, beads of sweat bursting across his forehead like the outside of a glass of an ice-filled beverage. His closed eyes would tighten and his mouth would spasm. It looked so painful. Then he'd hop up with his cock still heavy and sex-covered, walk over to the stereo and turn it off. He'd walk back to the sofa where her mother sat, take her glass of whatever and gulp the rest of it down. It was a very bizarre ritual.

"Can I have another glass of this?" Quinn asked the girl that wasn't the girl to ask.

"I'll send a waiter right over," the girl said, as if merely being asked to serve a drink had tested her patience. Quinn nodded, unconcerned about being corrected. That is, as long as she got her drink.

"So what are you doing after this?" Quinn asked Caesar quickly, now ready for some action. Caesar looked a little uneasy.

"Uh…" he hummed. "Don't know."

Quinn was a little uneasy now herself. Was she moving too fast? For a guy? The thought alone terrified her. She knew how boys liked to play the pursuer even when, or possibly even especially when, they were being pursued. But now she was horny. Images of Carmen fucking and her father fucking and one convoluted image that actually featured her father fucking Carmen: same sofa, Carmen ass-up, her father tapping heavy from behind and actually laughing, raced through Quinn's head. She wanted to feel something. She decided that something she wanted to feel was Caesar. Was he gonna deny her?

"What are your options?" Quinn asked.

"I gotta get home to my daughter," Caesar said, his eyebrows wrinkled. "My mother's watching her now, but she wants to go out later on. I told her I wouldn't be out late. It'd be kinda fucked-up if I left her hanging like that."

Quinn eyed Caesar as he eyed his plate. She hated him right then. All she wanted was some physical love. Who knew if she'd call him again or return his calls afterwards? Now he had to go and show that he had some sort of nobility to him. Right then, when the last thing in the world she wanted to do was to actually 'like' him.

H ow'd it go last night?" Carmen asked, her eyes about as wide as her legs were apart at that moment. The sight of the whole thing made Quinn dizzy.

She shrugged.

"I wanted to fuck him and he turned me down," Quinn said. Carmen made the expression of a two-year-old being taught algebra.

"He turned you down?"

Quinn shook her head.

"It was just…" she paused, thinking about the night before and the fantasies about her father and Carmen. "I just got horny and he had to go home and take care of his daughter."

"Maybe you were lonely," Carmen said, compassion heavy in her voice.

"Maybe," Quinn said, trying to shrug the idea off.

"You should have called me up," Carmen said cheerily. "I'd have kept you company. I wasn't doin' nothing."

Quinn deadpanned her.

"Called you up for what?" she asked, the accusation all but spoken.

Carmen frowned as if insulted.

"I don't know," she said a little hotly. "To talk. To hang out. To shoot pool. To bowl. To get some drinks. What? You think I just wanted you to call me up so you could fuck me?"

Quinn frowned, looked down and away.

"I'm sorry," she moaned. "I just…"

Carmen walked over and put her arms around her whispering in her ear.

"Don't worry about it," she said softly. "You don't have to fuck me. It was just an offer. Feel free to turn it down. I don't want you to feel uncomfortable around me just cause I want you to eat my asshole out."

"Thanks," Quinn said, with a bit of a perplexed frown on her face.

"You're welcome," Carmen said, before kissing Quinn between the ear and neck.

Her lips were so soft…

Quinn watched as Carmen's ass moved back to the front of the store. It was such a powerful weapon, that ass. It demanded attention. It could make a person forget about everything else in a room. It probably tasted sweet, Quinn thought, before chasing the thought out of her mind with something she considered to be morality. She shouldn't fuck another woman, she told herself. It didn't do anything but make you cum.

Quinn remembered Shortie and how she would bury her face in Quinn's pussy like she was fishing for something with her tongue. Quinn had never met anybody who could eat pussy like that girl and since Shortie was her first and only girl, Quinn was sure that it was a womanly trait, the ability to eat pussy like that. Shortie would suck her titties, pulling at her nipples with her teeth like she half wanted to snap them off like loose buttons on a coat. It would hurt so good. They rarely used a dildo. They were trying to forget about men, trying not to think about them or the need for them, a dildo, as pleasurable as it was when they did use it, seemed to be almost an accusation that something between them was, in fact, missing.

"Fuck men," Shortie would say, never telling Quinn that on Tuesdays when she would disappear for hours, she was disappearing to do just that. She had a boyfriend on the side. A stone-cold dyke like Shortie was sucking dick and taking it from behind from this faggot-looking dude that Quinn would have never even imagined let a woman get close enough to shampoo his hair let alone fuck him.

Quinn had come home that day, and there they were, Shortie and that dude, sitting on her sofa. Shortie, who even when she was standing up looked to be still sitting, had never been sexier. The lids of her eyes, which had always stayed half-closed, were now wide open. She was smiling. Quinn had never seen her smile. She looked at the dude. He was some dredlocked, simple-face dude with a wide mouth and dumpy disposition. He didn't even stand to greet her in her own apartment. The rude fucker.

"Quinn, let me explain," Shortie began, before Quinn had a chance to think about knives and any other household utilities she could fashion into weapons quickly.

"I love you," Shortie continued, her chestnut-colored skin never seeming as warm, her eyes never seeming as alive. "I wanna be with you for the rest of my life. But I also wanna have kids. I wanna have a family. I wanna give birth. I wanna be a mother."

"We could have adopted," Quinn said from her half-dream state, remembering right then with all the vividness of the present the night after that party in Chelsea when Shortie had pushed her into the cab. When she got her upstairs into her own apartment, Shortie had damn near raped Quinn, shoving her head up under Quinn's long skirt and sucking on her clit like it was a lemon. Now she was leaving. And she was leaving with a homo.

"I want the experience," Shortie said. And it was then, for the first time since they had become lovers, that Quinn could see her as a woman. And Shortie was such a pretty woman. The only thing that might have betrayed her intentions was the slight trace of a mustache. But her eyes, nose, cheekbones and form were all totally feminine. And they were totally beautiful. She wouldn't be back. This Quinn knew right then. She had what she wanted now. What she really wanted. All that time Quinn had thought that what Shortie really wanted was to be her, Quinn's, man. Now she realized that what Shortie really wanted, what she had always really wanted, was to be in a relationship with a man, but in the man's role. And this faggot was giving her just that.

"Get up, baby. Let's go," Shortie said softly to the man and he obliged, almost hopping at the command. If she hadn't been so sad, Quinn would have probably found it funny. Then they left. On their way out and as the door still hung open, the man peeked his head back in to add to Quinn:

"She really is a wonderful girl."

"I said 'come on'," Shortie snapped from the hallway and the man jumped like he had just heard the Word of God. The door slammed under its own weight and stayed closed.

But fucking Carmen wouldn't be like fucking Shortie, Quinn thought as she watched Carmen's ass at rest. Carmen was to be the girl, that much was certain. It was also one of the sexiest things about the proposition. All her life Quinn had been the girl, either with actual men or with a woman who wanted to have sex like she was a man. With Carmen, Quinn would have the balls. She'd eat the ass and probably the pussy too, while at the same time getting her titties licked and sucked by those lips which had just proven to be so soft...

Carmen must have felt her ass growing hot and she turned her head around to look at it before turning her whole body around to look at Quinn. By that time, Quinn was back at folding pairs of oversized boxer shorts looking innocently distracted.

"What was you doin'?" Carmen asked accusatorily.

Quinn looked up at her, looking at first confused, then annoyed for having to look up in the first place.

"You was doing something," Carmen continued.

Quinn wrinkled her lips.

"You want somebody to be doing something," she said. "Always wanna be the center of the universe."

"I am," Carmen said happily. "Everybody wants me."

How right she was, Quinn thought, remembering how that same day the week before when she'd been late, she went upstairs to see Bill. As it turned out, she wouldn't even be able to remember what had brought her upstairs that day. Bill's office was positioned to overlook the front of the store. The office door was locked, which was strange. Bill never kept the door locked. He had even given her and Carmen keys. So, Quinn thought, he just might not be there, even though she had seen him go in. Caught somewhere between wondering where he was and wondering what on earth he could be doing with the door locked, Quinn found herself, keys out, opening Bill's door.

Quinn thought he was on the phone at first, the way he spoke in hushed tones. But he kept saying 'Carmen'. Carmen was a level below them, standing near the counter at the front of the store. Carmen couldn't see into the office. Nobody could from inside the store. The glass was two-way; shaded if looked into from outside the office. But Quinn could see Carmen and, as it was, she was bent over the register adjusting the magazine rack. Quinn wondered absently why she just didn't walk around the counter to adjust the rack, and as she wondered she walked further and further into Bill's office, his whispers of Carmen's name becoming louder. She was almost side-by-side with Bill before she noticed that he was kneeling. Then she saw it. It looked to be almost green in his hands. Vein-laden and bulbous. If for complexion alone, Quinn would have mistaken it for a cucumber. One that her boss was rubbing like he was shaking dice.

"Aw Bill…" she moaned, finally realizing what was taking place.

"Quinn," Bill shouted, jumping in surprise, his

cucumber deflating in his hands. "I was, um…"

"Ill," Quinn moaned.

"Don't worry," he said quickly. "I never do this when I'm watching you."

"Thanks," Quinn deadpanned.

"I mean…" he paused, gathered himself, collected his breath then continued. "I don't know what it is about that girl. And that ass… I feel like such a pervert. And it's like she's teasing me with it too. Like, why does she have to lean all the way over the counter to straighten the magazine rack?"

Quinn didn't tell him that she had been wondering the same thing herself. Instead she said, "She can do whatever she wants. It's her body."

"I know, I know," Bill said, shaking his head as he stared through the glass at Carmen. Then he turned to Quinn. "What are you doing in here?" he asked.

Quinn froze. She had forgotten. But now it seemed like she found herself in a position to ask for just about anything.

"I want a day off," she said, the thought just occurring to her.

"What day?" Bill asked, as earnest as Quinn had ever seen him.

"Friday," Quinn said.

"Done," Bill said quickly.

"And don't ever question me or trouble me about my lateness again," Quinn continued.

"Done," Bill said quickly.

Quinn nodded to Bill, then to herself a little unevenly.

She wondered if she was letting him off the hook too easily. Or if this were a hook she'd ever really let him off. Either way, their relationship had now changed dramatically. And she was in charge of it.

Quinn returned to the floor of the store smiling. Carmen saw her out of the corner of her eye and smiled too. Quinn motioned with her eyes for Carmen to come to her. Carmen started right over, but Quinn shook her head and mouthed the words "in a minute" silently. Carmen nodded and pretended to go back to work. After about ten minutes had passed, Carmen began working her way to the back of the store, where Quinn was. She finally reached her co-worker's side.

"You know what Bill does up there when he's got the door locked?" Quinn asked with all the deliberate sloppiness of someone about to spill the beans.

"What?" Carmen asked quickly. "Jack off lookin' at my ass?"

Quinn's face went blank.

"How'd you know that?" she asked.

"Bill's been wantin' to fuck me since the first time he saw me," Carmen said as offhandedly as if she was predicting the next day's weather. "How do you think I got this job here? Why do you think my hours are arranged around my schedule at school?"

Quinn shook her head, confused.

"Why don't you just fuck him then?" she asked. "He's got a lot of money."

For the first time since they had begun talking as people who respected each other, even longer than they had been talking as friends, Carmen looked truly disappointed by something that Quinn had said.

"I don't like his movies," Carmen said simply.

"That's it?" Quinn asked.

"I don't like his clothes either," Carmen added.

Quinn was squinting and shaking her head, now almost violently confused.

"You don't like his movies or Big Niggaz clothes so you won't fuck him?" Quinn asked, as if simply repeating what she was being made to understand would help her understand it better.

"I don't think he's talented," Carmen said simply.

"Does Bill know that's why you won't fuck him?" Quinn asked. Carmen nodded. "How's he feel about that?" she asked. Carmen shrugged.

"He keeps telling me I'll like his next movie. 'Watch' he says, but he's been saying that for the last two years and I haven't liked shit. I didn't like any of the five that he made before I started working here either."

Quinn shook her head.

"So a guy could be ugly, have a little dick, can't dress, have bad breath and body odor, but if you think he's talented…"

"I'll fuck the shit out of him," Carmen said, finishing the thought. "Shit, a guy could be a girl. I wanna fuck you, remember?"

Quinn's face and whole body flushed. Still, something was gnawing at her.

Caesar came more to her as an image than an actual thought. Caesar had turned Carmen down. Well, at least that's what he said. If it was true, Quinn just had to fuck him. Absently, she put on hold her reasoning for this, knowing that there was something terrifyingly sexy about having the only man that the woman that could have any man in the world but one couldn't. She had to know for sure though and there was only one way to know without coming right out and asking.

"Was there ever anybody that you wanted to have sex with but couldn't?" Quinn asked Carmen, trying to sound as matter-of-fact as if she had just asked for a Spanish-flavored chicken casserole recipe.

Carmen was thoughtful.

"Yeah," she said, nodding her head unevenly. "This one dude that I met at a party one time with Steeze. I was gonna give him some but he said 'no'."

Quinn's eyes lit up. And for the rest of the day Carmen wondered what had suddenly made her co-worker so excited.

It was a raunchy-ass song and Quinn was getting horny as she wrote it. She really just wanted to fuck right then and anybody would have been in trouble if they had come to her door. Caesar, Carmen, Life, Shortie, maybe even Bill. No, not Bill and his cucumber dick. But just about anybody else.

'Belly Button'. That's what the song was called. And that's where she wanted it, all the way up to her belly button. Whatever they give her, be it tongue, dick, or as many fingers as could fit.

Being horny was always a mess to Quinn. Her part-time Catholic upbringing had always made her feel guilty for treating her body like it was something to be enjoyed and her mind like it was something to be explored. She remembered how when she was a girl, it would take her almost two hours to masturbate because every time her finger started getting good to her, she would pull it away knowing that anything that felt that good had to be a sin. Then she had sex for the first time. It was with this guy who acted like her already huge tits were punching and biting bags and her pussy was a refrigerator door to be continually opened and closed. He came screaming like he'd been shot, then hopped up, opened the door to the backseat, hopped back into the driver's seat and started the car. He was driving off before she had even pulled her panties all the way back up. So much for high school football stars, she thought at the time. She was sixteen.

Between then and up until the point where she was around twenty-three, Quinn had a steady stream of experiences, each different and each the same. All the men (Shortie and her didn't do it for the first time until she was twenty-eight) had treated her as if they were trying to lose themselves in her, or lose some part of themselves that they didn't like. Their lust? Quinn didn't know. But they'd be there, their heads buried into the pillow she lay on, their shoulders grinding into her chin, pounding inside her like if they hit her hard enough, they just might find what they were looking for. So much for basketball players, baseball players, soccer players, poets, drum majors, fraternity guys, the quiet, studious types, straight A students, the dangerous-gangster types and so on. Sure, a few were different. Some it seemed were actually intent on making her happy. Those few treated her body like she imagined that she would if given a chance to enjoy it externally. Her titties became ripe melons in their hands and her clitoris a drop of hot sauce that danced across their fingers and tongues. Of course, she would come to find out later that even the delicate handling of her body more often than not had ulterior motives. Too many times it seemed that Quinn would discover that many of the girls she had raved to about a certain brotha's techniques would find themselves in that same brotha's arms and being penetrated by that same brotha's intentions later on.

"It's a dirty game," Shortie had told her in college. And at the time Shortie was one of its best players. A 'girly-girl' still, getting sexed by men, or rather, sexing them, calling them 'bitches' and 'hoes' after she had finished with them. Shortie had been Quinn's hero since they had met during each other's freshman year. Shortie was from DC and since they were both going to school in Virginia, seemed to have a better understanding of the boys they were both continually encountering.

"These niggas ain't shit," Shortie would say. "They scared of themselves so you know they scared of some pussy."

Quinn would nod, but never really understand.

Shortie was hot, though, and all the niggas loved her. Her short, tight skirts and tight-ass thighs and ass were always on display, making Quinn occasionally wish for a harsh winter 'cause even then, she couldn't deny that Shortie's sex appeal did make her a little uncomfortable. But they were friends, swapping opinions and sometimes lovers, always at Shortie's suggestion.

"You should try him, girl. He's good," she'd say, and Quinn would nod later finding herself in bed with the boy and satisfied. And she would follow Shortie, sometimes just finding herself walking behind the girl, sure that something would happen just because of the company she was keeping. The girl was never boring. And the one thing Quinn hated perhaps more than anything else in the world was to be bored.

The lovers came and went, but Shortie didn't. When Quinn graduated with her useless degree in marketing and moved back to New York nodding and smiling at her parents like she really intended on doing something with the piece of paper that their money had earned her, Shortie came too. Shortie's degree was in broadcast journalism and she came to New York with Quinn despite the fact that nobody that either of them knew thought that the girl would find a job explaining the events of the day to anybody.

Then Shortie turned gay. It was funny as hell to Quinn at first because the men she had always chosen had been such thugs. It was as if she had been studying them to pick up techniques and now, having them figured, she was putting into practice what had been all along her master plan. Quinn would watch the girls that Shortie paraded around with and smile to herself. They were all so obviously confused. And Shortie would have them wrapped around her finger. Quinn would, at times, almost wish she was gay so that she could straighten Shortie's little ass out and show her that she was not, in fact, all that. But she didn't interfere. And when it came time for Quinn to make one of the seminal mistakes of her life and marry Cedric, Shortie stood in as her bridesmaid in an all-white blouse and lace, complete with a tight-ass black leather skirt.

Then that night happened. When Quinn thought about it, she realized what had sent her over the edge. It had been Joyce. She and Joyce were both singing back-up for Shaun's band on an R&B night at some terrible spot uptown. Before the show, Joyce had been just playing around singing 'Angel' by Anita Baker. But it had been the way she did it, fading into the song and then fading out, laughing and then growing serious, pensive, but never breaking the rhythm, the song naturally followed. She's just clowning around, Quinn thought terrified. What if she ever became really, really serious about singing? The thought was too much for Quinn's at-the-time delicate self-esteem to take. At the after-party later that night, Quinn drank way too much. So much that she was making everybody else uncomfortable, even Shortie who had come at the tail end of the show and gone with her to the party. Shortie had come with her new girlfriend. Some tall, dark-skinned girl named Marie with long legs, a tight, round ass and coffee-mug-sized breasts. Quinn didn't like Marie instantly.

At the party, Quinn was flirting so viciously with Shortie that Marie was at the point of tears. Everybody knew that Shortie was gay. They also knew that she and Quinn had known each other since college and were best friends. What few knew, perhaps only Shortie, was that Quinn and Cedric's marriage was now in the hands of lawyers and that the slightest thing, even something as trivial as hearing the voice of a woman who threatened to be a better singer than she was, could possibly send Quinn over the edge. And that was where she was right then.

"Come on girl, let's get out of here," Shortie said as she took a firm hold of her best friend's arm and pulled her from her slumped position in the chair to standing upright. "Marie, I'll call you later."

Marie nodded, but Shortie could tell that Marie knew as well as she did that that call was never gonna come.

"I love you," Shortie whispered with her head between Quinn's legs. "This is what I've always wanted. What I've always wanted." And it felt so good to feel and so good to hear that Quinn allowed herself to understand that a part of her had always wanted this too. Had always wanted Shortie. And now she had her.

It didn't take long for the rumors to start. Folks can spot love as easily as they can a car accident. And as the two friends now walked past old friends it was clear that they had become much closer friends than they had been before. Some shook their heads, some cheered openly, but all knew. Then for Shortie to go and pull the shit she had with that faggot-ass dredlocked nigga...

Quinn couldn't cum. It was useless. She couldn't focus on an image that in some way didn't involve guilt or memories. She pulled her hand away from herself, went into the bathroom and washed it off. She paused in front of the mirror, looking intently at herself as if she had just encountered somebody that owed her something. She shook her head and walked away. Whatever was owed, she didn't have on her right then. She went back to her chair at the desk where the last line of the song remained unwritten. 'Belly Button.'

Just fuck me. Hard, she wrote. Wasn't that what it was all about?

That had been the case with her ex-husband Cedric. Well at least it was the thing when he wasn't doing it hard. When he was, she wished he would slow down, calm down. He was always wrong. Doing the wrong thing at the wrong time the wrong way. But she had married him anyway and still couldn't give herself an answer as to why. Did she believe it was just time? Did she think her age, biological clock and friends dropping like flies to marriage or babies would leave her alone in the end looking silly? Did she really love Cedric that much? Did she love the music he made? Or was it that she loved the way he loved the music he made and hoped that eventually she would love the music she made the way he loved his? Whatever it was, it was wrong. And that same frustration he felt about his music whenever he played an 'off' note, and he was continually playing an 'off' note, he brought to their relationship whenever she was in an 'off' mood, and she was continually in an 'off' mood.

The violent jerk.

Over twenty thousand dollars in furniture was sacrificed to his rage and on the occasion that the gleam in his eye did seem at the point of overcoming him and she felt herself in some sort of physical danger, she would just go limp, submitting herself to him. For some reason, he could never do it, could never hit her. Though he'd come close a couple of times, the balled fist that his hand had been drawing back, way back, only to unravel again, and become a hand that usually ended up resting somewhere at the side of his beard. Cedric was not a good-looking man. But he was intense. And maybe that was it. Maybe it was his intensity that she had been attracted to. What on earth else could it have possibly been?

No, it wasn't about fucking hard, Quinn thought, as she erased the last line of the song. Shortie had never fucked her hard. Shortie had never really fucked her at all. Shortie had made love to her. So well that when she came and looked around, the walls seemed to be melting. She had loved Shortie and the way the girl could use all ten of her fingers, each like a different sexual instrument playing her body and making music so good that it was almost embarrassing. Her moans became a song with Shortie whispering "Keep singing", making her cum some more.

She should have known Shortie would leave her. Her goal the whole time they were together as lovers seemed to be to make Quinn happy. She almost never asked for anything in return. Who could continue indefinitely in a relationship like that?

Then came Life.

Quinn was definitely liberated by the time that nigga came around. She was giving orders like a drill sergeant.

"Nigga, eat this pussy and eat it well," she'd say, licking her lips like she would do it in his place if he couldn't do it right.

He'd comply, but his heart was rarely in it. Not that he wasn't trying, he just seemed a little afraid. It was as if he knew he had got in over his head simply by fucking with her and would be fighting a losing battle to keep her the entire time he was with her. He was right. She had been turned out, but not as much by the lesbian dynamic of her relationship with Shortie, by the pleasure of it. Shortie had given so genuinely. Anybody that gave with even a hint of an ulterior motive would be easy as hell to spot. And the fact that Life would always flop that dick of his in her face every time he finished eating her out was proof that he hadn't been doing what he'd been doing simply for her pleasure alone.

Now there was this new dilemma.

Who should she fuck, Carmen or Caesar? The problem with Carmen was that Quinn really didn't know if her time with Shortie had been a novelty or an alternative that was really innate within her. Sure, she had been attracted to women in the past. Women were beautiful. But the only one that she could have ever said with certainty that she wanted to have sex with had been Shortie. Now, she had done that. But Carmen was sexy as hell. And if there was a little bit of dyke in Quinn, it wasn't the tittie type, it was an ass type. And Carmen's ass... Man oh man, Carmen's ass... And yes, she knew she'd enjoy it. And yes, she knew that part of the reason that the attraction was so strong was because Carmen was attracted to her, thought she was talented in fact. But as far as Quinn was concerned, that door had opened and closed. If she opened it again, would she ever be able to close it?

The problem with Caesar was that she thought she liked him. That thing about his daughter had really touched her somewhere. Quinn had never really had sex with somebody she liked except Shortie. There had always had to be a little bit of animosity between her and her male sex partners for her to feel anything. She couldn't imagine smiling at the man she was about to command to 'fuck her hard' or taste her. It just didn't jive. Still, maybe she could find something to fight with him about right before they did it each time. Slap him or, maybe, call his daughter ugly or something. The thought made her laugh. It also opened another door. A door that closed the song 'Belly Button'.

She was nodding to herself as she sat back down at the desk. Shortie and Carmen couldn't be in this one, Quinn thought, shaking her head. Stuff like song lyrics were for 'so-called' traditional sexual partners. So with that in mind, Quinn chuckled a little to herself as she erased a line, and followed it with the following two:

Give it to me till you get in trouble with it
Then pull it out so you can leave a puddle in it.

That should send 'em home fuckin', she thought with a smile, imagining her audience in a hurry to leave right after she had sung the last note. The funny thing was, she wasn't thinking about herself at all anymore.

It was rare that she saw her parents in the crowd and Quinn was always a little uncomfortable when they were there. Her mom would always look too eager while her dad would always look too uptight. What a time to debut 'Belly Button', she thought. But she was a singer, meaning this was what she did. They'd have to understand.

The drummer had come bringing a pound of herb and about eight pills of Ex, all of which he had gotten from Life. Her regular piano player was back so she didn't have to worry about the ranting of that asshole: Phil Flarn, as well as the regular sax and trumpet men. Even the shock of seeing her parents, who hadn't called to tell her that they were coming up from their new home in Maryland hadn't completely thrown Quinn for a curve. Everything looked like it might go okay.

"Nah," Quinn said, waving off both the weed and the Ex. The drummer looked disappointed to the point of being insulted.

"You don't wanna get high?" he asked, incredulous.

Quinn shook her head.

"Not tonight," she said. "My parents are here. We're probably gonna go out somewhere after the show."

"Girl, your parents don't know you're a drug addict?" the drummer mocked.

Quinn wrinkled her lips.

"You better stop living in denial," the drummer continued.

"Do your parents know you're gay?" Quinn asked.

"Hell no," the drummer laughed. "Shit, I brought my lover home for the Christmas holidays and had to tell my parents he was my psychiatrist."

"Your psychiatrist?"

"Yeah, when my mother caught me lying on the couch with his dick in my mouth I had to tell her that we were in a session."

"What did you tell her his dick was?" Quinn asked, incredulous.

"My cell phone," the drummer said.

Quinn moaned, but it wasn't as if she didn't understand. When she had married Cedric she didn't try to imply to her father that her husband would be her first lover, but she wouldn't have tried to persuade him otherwise if that was what he believed. Quinn's mother was a little more open-minded, but not much more. It was almost funny. The couple that had drank and Al Green-ed themselves to death on the sofa right in front of her eyes couldn't seem to imagine that their daughter would have a sex life. They would have probably never allowed themselves to take the blame for how distorted it had become. Not that Quinn voiced any regrets, but she certainly didn't get the impression that sex was something that was supposed to be enjoyed by both parties from her parents. And now that they had become older, her parents hid so far behind the walls, covenants and ideologies of the church that it was hard for Quinn to imagine that they fucked at all anymore. Quinn's father certainly didn't look like they did. And as far as drugs were concerned…

"Wait a minute," Quinn said to the drummer, her eyebrows wrinkled in thought.

"What's up, girlie?" he asked.

"Sell me two of those Ex pills," she said.

"Two?" the drummer asked incredulous. "You plannin' on falling in love tonight or something?"

"Or something," she said, then handed the drummer a crisp fifty dollar bill in exchange for the pills.

"That was a good set, honey," Maxine Carr said to her daughter from across the table afterwards.

Quinn smiled simply because her mother knew enough to use the word 'set'.

"Yeah, what was up with the song 'Belly Button'?" Greg Carr asked, his face earnest.

"It's just a song, daddy," Quinn said innocently.

"Yeah, well I don't like it," Greg said, his earnestness giving way to borderline aggression.

Quinn shrugged, the corner of her eye catching her mother's hand patting her father's hand sternly.

"When are you gonna make an album?" Maxine asked.

Quinn shrugged again.

"I just did a song on Shaun's upcoming album," Quinn began. "Remember Shaun?"

Maxine nodded unevenly.

"Light-skinned, tubby, sickly looking guy, right?" she

asked. "With a nose like a labrador retriever?"

Quinn nodded.

"Yeah," she said. "Him. I just did this song on his album which'll be out in the summer and I'm supposed to be doing a couple of songs on the soundtrack to Bill's new movie, so we'll see."

Maxine nodded slowly. Greg looked unimpressed.

"You need to get a job," he said, in the same tone he used to criticize 'Belly Button'.

"I've got a job, daddy," Quinn said patiently.

Greg wrinkled his lips.

"A real job," he moaned. "A job that we spent all that money on a goddamned degree for."

"Greg..." Maxine said, checking her husband.

"Mom..." Quinn said, checking her mother.

Their eye contact became three-way.

Quinn wanted to laugh. For as long as she'd been singing in this joint, she had no idea that the food was so good. She usually went somewhere else after a set to eat. But her parents had been snacking there all throughout the set and when she suggested that they leave to get some food, Greg with his characteristic unwillingness to change asked, "What's wrong with the food here?" It turned out to be a good question.

Maxine had been both noting and counting all the people that came up and patted her daughter on the back about her performance as well as mentally processing all the comments (good, bad, and indifferent) about the way she sang. People really seemed to think that Quinn had talent. It felt good knowing that she hadn't been biased all those years simply because Quinn was her daughter.

"People seem to really like you, baby," Maxine said, thinking of some of the praises now.

Quinn nodded unevenly.

"I don't think anybody understands me, though," she said.

"The best are never understood," Maxine breathed hotly. "Billie Holiday, Toni Morrison, Dorothy Dandridge…"

"Redd Foxx," Greg interrupted to say.

Both his wife and daughter turned to him, deadpanned.

"What?" Greg asked, incredulous. "Redd was the best."

Maxine shook her head.

"You're in good company," she continued.

"Damn right," Greg continued.

And Quinn could tell that the time was near.

"Have you guys been over by the bar?" she asked as innocently as she could.

"What's at the bar?" Greg asked, always suspicious.

Quinn shrugged.

"It's just a beautiful bar and the bartender's friendly," she said off-handedly.

Maxine seemed to sense something. She frowned a little and wrinkled her lips.

"C'mon Greg," she said beginning to stand. "It's obvious our daughter wants us to go over by the bar."

Quinn was relieved if embarrassed by the fact that her mother knew she was up to something.

"I just don't understand why we're going over there," Greg began, standing anyway. "I mean, a waitress'll bring us our drinks over here…"

Quinn was faced with a dilemma. The pills certainly wouldn't dissolve in their drinks, but given their food choices, Maxine's fettuccini and Greg's chicken parmesan, always chicken parmesan, she couldn't think of a place to hide them. She decided to risk it, stuffing a whole one in the middle of her father's chicken, while breaking up the other pill and sprinkling the crumpled contents into Maxine's fettuccini and mixing it up. She then turned and watched her parents at the bar. As expected, her father had found something to argue with the bartender about and it wasn't long before both Greg and Maxine were headed back over to their daughter's table.

"What was that all about?" Quinn asked, once they returned. Maxine exhaled deep as she sat down.

"The bartender's a Knicks fan," she said.

"Dumb mothafucka," Greg fumed.

"Daddy," Quinn moaned.

"I ain't hungry no more," Greg said, pushing his plate away.

Quinn became nervous.

"Daddy will you please eat your food?" she half-demanded, half-pleaded.

"Yeah Greg," Maxine said, twirling a fork through her own plate. "The fettuccini's good."

With that, she scooped up several large twists and stuffed them into her mouth.

Mom always comes through, Quinn thought with a smile.

"Un-uh," Greg moaned. "Like I always say, 'If you can't

do chicken parm right, you can't do shit'."

"Just like that movie," Maxine and Quinn said simultaneously, shaking their heads at the same time too and never looking more like mother and daughter than right at that exact moment.

"Daddy, please eat your food," Quinn began again. "It's complimentary."

"It's free?" Greg asked animatedly.

Quinn nodded.

"Shit, why didn't you say that in the first place?" With that, he dug in.

Quinn was smiling ear to ear.

The drummer stopped by the table on his way out the door. He had been sitting, eating and having drinks at a table all the way across the room. He kissed Quinn on the cheek and whispered in her ear, "You start on your fantasy ride?"

Quinn shook her head, grinning through closed lips. "They did," she whispered back.

"Oooooooohhhhh," the drummer moaned, then left with a boy that Quinn would have never in a million years imagined... Never in a million years...

"This is pretty good," Greg said between chews and Quinn knew it was the freeness of the food, not the Ecstasy that was affecting his judgment. The Ex wouldn't be kicking in for at least another half-hour.

Everybody had finished eating before Greg. This made sense, being that he had been the last one to start. He had judged the parmesan from its smell, never bothering to taste it, before becoming convinced that it was good from its lack of a price. Now he was finished and his standing up signaled to his wife and daughter that he was ready to leave. They stood with him.

"I really liked that," Greg said, his smile genuine and what looked like tears beginning to form in his eyes. "It was really good." He reached into his back pocket producing his wallet.

"I think I'll leave a tip for the waiter."

Quinn and Maxine looked on in shock. Greg leaving money when he didn't have to? This had to be an act of God.

"Matter of fact," Greg continued, "I wanna leave something for the cook too. Max baby, you got like an envelope or something to write on so that I can leave two tips, one for the waiter and one for him to give to the cook."

"You don't have to leave a tip for the cook," Maxine said patiently.

"Yeah, but I wanna thank him," Greg said, seeming tragically disappointed.

"Then just go to the kitchen and thank him, baby," Maxine said softly.

Greg walked off. Maxine turned to Quinn.

"What did you put in our food?" she asked simply. "Ecstasy?"

Quinn's eyes went wide.

"Mommy," she pleaded, unsure of whether to be more shocked by the fact that her mother had accused her of such a thing or the fact that her mother was right.

Maxine shook her head.

"I hope your father can handle it," was all she said.

"Good night everybody," Greg cheered, re-emerging from the kitchen. Hands, glasses and moans went up for Greg as he crossed the floor back over to his wife and daughter.

"Y'all ready?" he asked, wrapping his arms around them both.

"Yeah, daddy," Quinn said softly.

Maxine just nodded. And off they went.

Greg's hand was heavy on the small of Quinn's back as he gently pushed her towards then through the door. It was really close to her ass and if he hadn't been her father, she would have been a little suspicious. Still, it was good to feel her father. His mood seemed like a light within him turned up to full wattage. Maxine seemed a little off. She wasn't as loving as Greg yet. The Ex was taking a little longer for her, Quinn theorized. Plus, she knew what she was on. That could have also been fostering the delay. Still, Quinn felt as if she had done the right thing and floating with her father, who really did seem to be walking without his feet touching the ground, through the streets of midtown Manhattan. It was like touring a mythic city with a king and she was his princess. It was funny. Her parents had taken the pills and she was sharing in the euphoria.

People passing on the street seemed to notice something in Greg, perhaps his light. He nodded and winked, smiling at random intervals, turning the city on with himself. It was really a sight for Quinn who was used to the perpetual scowl her father kept for strangers and the harsh words that seemed ready for even someone attempting to exchange pleasantries. When they arrived at the parking garage, Greg actually made small talk, thanking the Saudi attendant for 'watching over their family chariot' and tipping him a Greg-unthinkable twenty dollars. They all hopped in, Greg in the driver's seat, Maxine and Quinn in the back.

"Oh, I'm chauffeuring?" Greg asked through a chuckle.

"Yeah, I wanna talk to Quinn for a while?" Maxine said.

"Talk to our daughter, baby," Greg sang, as he turned the key in the ignition, pulled the lever of the car into 'drive' and navigated the lengthy Lincoln out into the narrow Manhattan avenues.

"Do you like your father like this?" Maxine whispered to Quinn.

Quinn frowned.

"You don't?" she asked, almost incredulous.

Maxine shook her head.

"I just know the downside," she said simply.

"What downside?"

"He's not gonna be like this tomorrow."

"Then enjoy him tonight," Quinn said. And it was like she could see it in her mother's eyes. The Ecstasy had kicked in.

"Yeah," Maxine said, first nodding, then nodding and smiling. "Yeah," she said again, nodding and smiling wider.

"Yeah," Quinn said, nodding and smiling a little herself.

Her father was standing before her naked. Erect. Quinn was just coming from her bathroom, going into her living room to offer her parents amenities for the evening; sheets and a comforter for the bed that folded out of the sofa, perhaps a nightgown for her mother and a heavy pair of flannel boxer shorts for her father. She had stopped dead in her tracks. They looked at each other, father and daughter, their eyes locking as if being joined from the distance.

"Daughter…" Greg said beginning to smile. Quinn blinked hard, shook her head, a cursory glance along her father's body. It was hard. Greg's body, that is. Surprisingly so. At fifty, he was fitter than many of the boys she had slept with that were half his age. She had tried not to look at his member but, failing, fought with herself to restrain the inevitable comparisons that would come when she remembered some of the others she had seen. This was her father, her morality screamed, as she found herself comparing his dick to Life's, to Cedric's, to Bill's…

"Your mother and I were just about to make love," Greg said. "Would you like to join us?"

"Ugh," Quinn moaned as Maxine's head rose above the side of the sofa, shocking her to shame that now her mother had caught her staring at her naked father. Greg laughed, his tightening stomach causing his member to bounce up and down where it was.

"I don't mean do you wanna fuck us," he continued. "I just mean that love is a spiritual thing and that it should be shared with anybody you feel it towards. Certainly, you've seen people making love before…" Images of porno movies gone by flooded Quinn's memory with quick, violent scenes of sex. "They were probably the wrong people too," Greg continued. "I just wanted you to watch it being done the right way." Quinn sneaked a quick glance at Maxine who now had her chin resting on the arm of the sofa and was smiling at her.

"He's right, baby," Maxine said, now rising, shocking Quinn again with her own nakedness. Her tits are still bigger than mine, Quinn thought with a start, remembering a time when all she had wanted was titties as big as her mother's. And they're still firm, Quinn thought, shaking her head. But Maxine had an ass too. And that's what Quinn saw next as Maxine turned and began backing up towards Greg.

What's about to happen here?

Quinn squinted, turning away watching her father slide into her mother. They had both been looking at her the entire time.

"Watch baby," Maxine called out softly and as Quinn turned to follow her mother's command she noticed that Maxine's eyes had closed and her mouth had opened into an almost vicious curl. "Uhh," she moaned, her ass arched high into the air, her fingers digging deep into the arm of the sofa. Greg's front teeth rested lightly on his extended tongue. It was as if he was swinging, really. The way he swayed, first down, then up and in. He really seemed to be enjoying himself. He was popping Maxine's ass upward, lightly tapping it, with each rise in her thighs, her fingers beginning to dig a little more. He was getting all the way under her, then all the way into her. It was like a ballet and were it not for the light applause of Maxine's breasts, Quinn might have become distracted enough not to realize that her parents were fucking in front of her. But they were fucking. And the fire in her own pelvis made her ashamed. She closed her eyes and began using her hand to extinguish it.

"We turning you on, baby?" Maxine asked, shocking Quinn's eyes wide. She snatched her hand away from herself. "Don't be ashamed," Maxine continued, as if reading her daughter's mind. "This is what's supposed to be turning you on."

"That's right," Greg said as he took a particularly big swing. "Not some perversion. Love. Love is what's supposed to be turning you on."

"Does your father have a big dick?" Carmen asked, eyes wide.

"Carmen," Quinn's expression was sour, as if she'd just been hit in the mouth with an open-ended lemon.

"Ooh…" Carmen moaned, her hands now on either side of her waist sliding down to her hips. "Your father? I bet he'd be good." Carmen was in her own world now. Her eyes were closed, her mouth was open and her thumbs were on the insides of her tight black stretch pants, gradually beginning to pull them down.

"Ooh…" Carmen moaned again as Quinn looked on, astonished but afraid to say anything for fear that she would stop. She had just reached the top of her divide when a sound similar to an explosion startled both her and Quinn back into the immediate.

"What was that?" Carmen asked, pulling her hands out of her pants, but not pulling them back up. Quinn found it hard to look away.

"I think it was something in Bill's office," Quinn said, her eyes still glued to the top of Carmen's backside.

"Bill's office?" Carmen asked nervously.

Quinn looked up into her eyes.

"Yeah..." she said, as an idea began forming in her mind. Carmen pulled her pants back up. Quickly, Quinn climbed the stairs, used her keys and opened Bill's locked office door. There Bill was; tangled in the wiring of the floor lamp which lay stretched across his body and the track lighting its fall had apparently knocked from the ceiling. His dick was out, of course.

He didn't even say anything as Quinn walked over and began to untangle him. He just lay there with his mouth open, shaking his head, his eyes wide in amazement. When Quinn had finally freed him, he gently tucked his dick in, climbed to his feet and sat down in his office chair. Quinn looked at him like one might a child continually caught with his hand in the cookie jar, turned and began walking out of the office.

"Quinn?" his voice came from over her shoulder.

She stopped. Then turned.

"What, Bill?" she asked with the voice of a mother whose patience had been tried one too many times.

"What were you two talking about?"

What surprised Quinn the most had been the morning. She had been so sure as she climbed into bed and rubbed herself both harder and more vigorously than perhaps she ever had, that the next morning between herself and her parents would be the most difficult thing she'd ever endure in her life. If Greg or Maxine were anything like her, the Ex would make them dog-tired, perhaps even throwing off their sleeping rhythms for the next week or so. Also, the embarrassment she was sure her parents would both feel for fucking in front of their daughter would probably be enough to put the whole family in therapy. But when Quinn woke up and walked towards the living room, peeking around the corner of her bedroom door just to see if Greg and Maxine were still asleep, she was surprised to see her father both standing and, this time, fully dressed.

"Hey baby-girl," Greg cheered, as he had years before and not in a long time since. He was smiling a genuinely happy smile.

"Hey baby," Maxine called from her seat on the sofa.

"Hi guys," Quinn said, rubbing her forehead with her hand, pretending to have an itchy eye but really just trying to hide her face as she made her way to the bathroom. She brushed her teeth slowly, checking her face for signs that thirty years of age was now suddenly making her old. She thought about her mother's body the night before and wondered what to attribute it to. Sure, her mother had done those Jane Fonda workout tapes fifteen years earlier and jumped and sweated with just about every early morning show on ESPN, but how did she keep those big-ass titties still swinging high? She decided to pull her aside and ask her after breakfast, which she decided right then and there that she'd make for her parents. It would be the least that she could do.

Quinn walked out of the bathroom and decided not to be surprised to see her mother's leg bent with her foot resting on the arm of the sofa, her father on his knees, pants around his ankles, pumping slowly back and forth towards the origin of his wife's leg.

"Back at it, huh?" Quinn asked flatly.

"Yeah…" Greg panted, beads of sweat heavy on his forehead. "And it don't have nothing to do with that shit your mother told me you slipped us last night. I just genuinely love this woman."

"That's good, Dad," Quinn moaned. "Just please try to cum inside her. It costs a fortune to have the pillows from that sofa cleaned."

"Will do, baby-girl."

"My mother and father," Quinn said to Bill.

"That made Carmen start pulling her pants down?" Bill asked incredulously.

"You should see my father's dick."

Bill's expression was somewhere between surprise and interest. Quinn decided to leave him with that thought.

"So push-ups, huh?" Carmen asked, once Quinn had returned downstairs.

"That's what she said." Quinn said. "She said it keeps the muscles tight." Carmen shrugged.

"Well, I don't have to really worry about that," she said wistfully. "I don't have too many titties."

"Yeah, but you gotta keep that ass together," Quinn warned.

"I already do."

"How?"

"You should see me," Carmen said, becoming
animated. "I run five miles a day. I bike ride. I jump rope.
This ass is gonna be hard and firm until I'm seventy."
Quinn was nodding but her mind had returned to her own
situation. Everybody seemed to have a plan but her.
Carmen, as crazy as she seemed, was studying for her
Master's degree in Journalism at nearby NYU. And the girl
was a genuinely good writer too. So good in fact, that
Quinn imagined her in a continual state of masturbation
given the girl's lust for the talented. And Carmen had
Steeze. There was just no substitute for having found your
life-partner, nigga, bitch, homo-friend, or whatever the hell
you were looking for. Her mother and father would always
be together and if the night before was any indication, their
love life seemed to be rejuvenated. Even matching maniacs
like that asshole: Phil Flarn and Joyce had found each
other. Why was God making things so hard for her?

"Your time is coming," Carmen said without looking
up from some bandannas she was folding in the front of
the store. Quinn looked at her, noticing that her eyes were
still lowered towards her work. She nodded, knowing that
Carmen couldn't see her and mouthed a 'Thank you',
knowing that Carmen couldn't hear it.

So what's the deal with Quinn?" Phil Flarn asked, lying flat on his back on his bed, his eyes on the game being played on the television before him.

"Don't know all the angles yet," said Caesar, sitting upright on the edge of his bed, his eyes rotating between the game and his daughter, who kept coming into then leaving his room with improvements on her homework.

"I think she's gonna let me give her the seven-footer though."

"Oh," Phil Flarn laughed suddenly. "The guy loves pulling out his Larry Johnson and trying to share it with people." They both collapsed laughing on their respective beds, each needing to readjust the position of the phones in their hands.

"What was the dinner date like?" Phil Flarn asked, becoming sober again. "Was she giving you rhythm, what?"

"She was like, 'back-and-forth'," Caesar said offhandedly. "At one point, it seemed like her mind was somewhere else. Then at the end, it seemed like she might wanna take me back to her crib and break me off that night."

"Why didn't you go?"

"My mom had to work and I had to come home and take care of Champagne."

"Oh. How is the baby-bam?"

"She's straight," Caesar said. "She's up to second grade English already and she's only in the first grade."

"Told you that girl was smart."

"What's up with your lady?" Caesar asked.

"Joyce?" Phil Flarn asked rhetorically. "That girl's a fuckin' nut."

"Sounds like the pot calling the kettle a 'nigger'," Caesar laughed.

"I guess so," Phil Flarn said offhandedly. "But, like, the other night, I was explaining to her daughter all the finer points of *The Mack* and Joyce kept getting all mad and shit."

"How old is her daughter?"

"Three."

"And you were showing her *The Mack*?"

"Yeah," Phil Flarn said.

"With all the nude scenes and cursing?"

"Yeah," Phil Flarn said evenly. "Her daughter's smart. She was getting it. She laughed at all the Richard Pryor parts and everything."

"Did you at least cover her eyes during the sex scenes?" Caesar asked.

"Why?" Phil Flarn asked, incredulous. "Nobody covered mine!" Caesar shook his head. He had known Phil Flarn since he had been born. Phil's mother was his godmother. But at no point during their entire thirty-year relationship did Phil Flarn cease to amaze him.

"Yo, I'm gettin' ready to go, man," Phil Flarn was saying to him now.

"On your way to Joyce's?" Caesar asked slyly.

"Of course," Phil Flarn cheered. "Hold it down. You gonna watch the rest of this game?"

"Yeah."

"Tell me who won."

They hung up.

Caesar had been thinking a lot about Quinn since their date. More than he had even wanted to admit to himself. And it went beyond her titties. The girl was just plain... mysterious. There was something about her that extended beyond the physical. There was something soulful about her. Something spiritual. Something that Caesar felt that if he explored fully, it could open up some answers to some questions he had always had about himself.

Caesar had always been a patient man. Sure, he usually took the pussy that presented itself to him, but as far as life choices were concerned, he was always a little hesitant to alter things that seemed to be working. He had only been away from his hometown for an extended period once and that was during the two years he spent south at a black college before running out of money. All the twenty-eight years before and since had been spent right there in New London, New York. For the past ten years he'd worked at the same hospital as laboratory technician and was gradually working his way up the corporate ladder, promotion after promotion, raise after raise until finally, he considered himself living comfortably. Perhaps one day, he'd start a business of his own. Whatever the case, he'd certainly have enough money to send his daughter, Champagne, away for all four years of college and a degree.

His buddy Phil Flarn, by contrast, had lived in Chicago, New Orleans, San Diego and Portland, Maine. Phil had been an accountant, a grocery store shelf stock-guy, a bus driver, and a garbage man. Phil had been married, annulled, arrested, convicted and addicted to marijuana, chocolate and beer. It had been no wonder that Caesar and Phil Flarn had always got along so well. They needed each other.

Caesar had always been a big fan of Phil Flarn's piano playing. What had been a hobby for Phil, Caesar had always tried to convince him was good enough to make a career. It had been Caesar who had talked Phil into quitting his job as an accountant and joining the first band that would hire him. When Phil got his first gig as a piano player, Caesar was there.

Phil Flarn's move to Brooklyn had been directly from Portland, Maine, a location Caesar had no idea how Phil found himself in. Phil Flarn had seemed to gather himself a little up there. He had seemed to get himself together. At least enough to realize that the last thing he wanted to do was live in Portland, Maine. So Phil Flarn returned to New York, though this time not to New London, to Brooklyn, and began putting to use a college degree in accounting he had miraculously earned, despite continually finding himself under the feminine wiles of anything with a pussy during his less than illustrious college career. Caesar would go to check him out on occasion in Brooklyn under the guise of simply hanging out with his dawg, but more accurately to check and see if Phil Flarn was remaining sane. It was lifetime work, Caesar acknowledged to himself. But at least it was cheaper for Phil Flarn than a therapist.

Caesar remembered how anxious Phil Flarn had been before his first gig. How he had sweated bullets and even, at one point, insisted that Caesar impersonate and play for him. Caesar did play a little piano. Phil Flarn had insisted to him that he was good. But Caesar knew that if Phil Flarn were to ever become a piano player, he'd have to do it that night. So, positioning himself in the rear of the club, he sat back and listened as Phil Flarn played jazz piano for a bunch of white boys singing folk songs. It was terrible. The sound of the piano was like a cry for help being almost drowned out by a bunch of screams of apathy. Luckily, somebody heard that cry and, soon, Phil Flarn was moving on up.

The clubs got better and so did the parties. Phil Flarn, who had been a complete no-name in the beginning, was gradually beginning to get some of the recognition Caesar had always believed his friend deserved. Caesar didn't come to see his friend play at every club or attend every party with him, but when he sensed his presence was needed, he made sure he was there. Such was the case the night he met Quinn.

Caesar had always been popular with the ladies. He knew all about his eyes and he kept himself in the kind of shape that a slim man with a slim build should: tight and together. The women had come and gone, some staying, some making a mark of some kind, one, in the most improbable night of passion, giving him a daughter that he was now raising with the help of his mother, all he was appreciative of. He liked the man he had become. And he knew enough to attribute at least some of it to the women he had known. Of course, he had regrets.

Julie, the tall, dark-skinned Haitian girl, also from New London, that he had met while she was in her sophomore year at North Carolina and had given him perhaps the most exciting two years of his life. He would drive down to see her on weekends and chill while campus celebrities and basketball players gave him the sort of looks that made him realize that folks had wanted to know who he was because they had wanted to know why they were unsuccessful in getting with Julie. He had liked her because she was fine and smart. She had liked him because he was smart and fine. But they had clashed on issues as simple as what each planned to do the next day, so the distant future was always more of a disagreement than a promise. It just sort of stopped: the relationship. Neither had the heart to end it, but neither had the strength to feed it.

Then there was Toni. Toni was from New London too. She and Caesar had known each other their whole lives and had actually lived next door to each other for almost twenty years. At five years old Caesar had moved from his first apartment in downtown New London to the projects of middle New London before moving back downtown into the house that his great-uncle had left for him and his mother when he died. It was while back downtown that

Caesar and Toni first noticed things about each other that had somehow escaped each of them while they had been neighbors and friends. Yes, Toni thought, he is fine and not just generically because of his eyes and tight frame. He's smart too. If he'd had the money for college, he'd probably be a businessman or something by now. And yes, Caesar thought, those appendages that were so cute when they were developing and forming have left this girl with an almost cartoon-like caricature of a body. This short girl with a beautiful-ass face that laughs at his jokes and doesn't talk during movies had a beach ball for an ass and two rugby balls for titties. They had to do something. Tragically for Caesar, that something was everything but head.

"You mean you're never gonna suck my dick?" Caesar asked after the first six months of a nearly perfectly blissful relationship. It wasn't that Caesar had missed blow jobs; yet. The sex had been incredible. But he could foresee a day, like a man who eats his favorite food each day, every day, that he would get tired of just sex alone.

"Un-uh," she had said, making a face as if he had just suggested that she eat dog waste.

"Even after we're married?" he asked, his eyes wide beneath troubled eyebrows. They had discussed marriage already. Things had been that good. Toni shook her head.

"Why not?" he asked, even though he had already decided in his own mind that no answer would be good enough.

"It's against my religion," she said simply.

"Against your *religion?*" he asked, incredulous.

"Yes, my God teaches us that only food should be eaten," she said.

"I'm not asking you to bite it off and chew it," he screamed.

She shook her head.

It was hard after that. They tried, but it was as if a part of the relationship had died that day. She couldn't believe that he would let something as insignificant as blow-jobs interfere with what promised to be a lifetime of happiness. He couldn't believe that she'd never suck his dick.

"Daddy?" Champagne called out, bringing Caesar back to the present. He turned to look at the five-year-old girl whose face and eyes were his.

"Somebody named Quinn is on the phone," she continued. And for the first time since hanging up with Phil Flarn, Caesar smiled.

Carmen had worried her to death. The girl had even listened in on the phone call, going 'awwwww' when Quinn had asked Caesar what he was doing and he said teaching his daughter long division.

"Why didn't you fuck him?" Quinn had asked right after hanging up the phone, the day and time of their next date secured.

"I wanted to," Carmen said without missing a beat.

Quinn had explained to Carmen who Caesar was and Carmen had remembered him. Quinn had figured that it was better to tell Carmen then than have Caesar show up somewhere to meet her and have Carmen find out that way. Quinn wasn't one for surprises. Plus, there was a little bit of pride knowing that a guy that Carmen had offered that big, wonderful ass to had turned it down in favor of the possibility of positioning himself between her own narrow hips.

"You gonna fuck him?"

Quinn looked troubled.

"Don't know," she said pensively. "This weekend doesn't look good."

"Why not?"

"Something else might happen," Quinn said simply.

Carmen looked confused at first. Then her eyes widened.

"Oh..." she moaned. Then she shrugged. "So what?" she asked. "You never fucked a guy on your period?"

"Not the first time," Quinn said, frowning at what she was sure to be an admission from Carmen.

"That's the best time," Carmen cheered. "You get to see just how nasty a nigga is. And if he'll eat you out..."

"Ugh..." Quinn moaned. "You let guys do that to you when you're on your period?"

"Let 'em?" Carmen asked, just as incredulous. "Shit, a lot of 'em insisted."

Quinn rushed towards the very back of the store, to the bathroom holding her stomach. When she got there and opened the door, she turned on the light, lifted up the toilet seat and stood there, dry-heaving into the bowl. Nothing would come. She turned out the light and just stood there in the dark, disgusted. Why did Carmen do that to her? How did Carmen do that to her? Did she wanna know how nasty Caesar was? Certainly she did, but not initially. What if he was a real freak? She pictured him, his pretty eyes following his head as it traveled along the path down her stomach towards an area that she would have already warned him to be quarantined. What would she think of him after he had done it? What would she think of herself after she had allowed him to do it? For some reason, time always seemed to be the answer. Like, maybe if she had known Caesar for years or had been with him for years and she had wanted him to do that to her or he had wanted to do it himself, it wouldn't have seemed so horrific. But the first time? Quinn shook her head.

"Nah," she said aloud, in the bathroom by herself with the lights out. If he could do that to her on their first time, who knew what he had done to other girls?

Quinn washed her hands. That was something her mother had always taught her made you feel cleaner. Frequently after conversations with Carmen, she had felt the need to feel cleaner. When she walked back out on to the floor, Alanda was handling a pair of jeans from a stack that Quinn had folded not a half an hour before. She hadn't seen Alanda since the night that she had met Caesar. Alanda rarely made public appearances.

"Alanda?" Quinn said, hoping the tone of pleasant surprise in her voice overrode the tone of embarrassment she knew her voice always held whenever one of her friends from the music world came to visit her at her day job.

"What's up, girl?" Alanda asked, returning the jeans to the stack. "Your work?" she asked, her eyes glancing quickly towards the jeans.

Quinn attempted an unsuccessful smirk. She met Alanda near the jeans and they hugged, pecking each other lightly on the cheek.

"You're a perfectionist," Alanda continued. "I could tell if it was you that pumped a gallon of gas." Quinn attempted an unsuccessful chuckle. "How's the album coming?" Alanda asked.

"It's coming," Quinn said nervously. "What brings you around?"

"Oh…" Alanda said, her eyes for the first time really resting on Quinn's. "I heard that song you did on Shaun's album. It's crazy."

"Thank you," Quinn said, smiling humbly.

"I know this rapper guy that's looking for somebody to do some background vocals for a single he's getting ready to drop," Alanda continued. "Now, I know you're a big jazz vocalist and you probably feel that hip-hop is beneath you, but I let him hear that song and he really wants you on the single."

Quinn was skeptical.

"I don't really do hip-hop, girl," she said, her face wrinkled. "I mean, I like it. I respect it as an art form. But I'm not really a hip-hop singer."

"That's what I told him," Alanda said with a sigh. "He thought you still might be willing to do it, considering."

"Considering what?"

"Considering how much he'll pay, considering who he is?"

"How deep into his pockets is he willing to go?" Quinn asked, now a little intrigued.

"Seventy-five thousand plus a point for the session," Alanda said simply.

"Seventy-five thousand?" Quinn repeated.

Alanda nodded.

"And a point?" Quinn asked.

Alanda nodded again.

"Damn, I've never recorded a hip hop song where I got royalties..." Quinn said, more to herself than to Alanda. "Who's the guy?"

"Bay-B," Alanda said simply.

If a name had ever almost caused a spontaneous orgasm...

"I love him," Quinn said, as if she were breathing the emotion through her words.

"We all do," Alanda said simply.

"He's so clever," Quinn continued.

Alanda nodded. There was pause, filled with the time Alanda allowed Quinn to let it all sink in.

"So I can take that as a 'yes'?" Alanda asked finally.

Quinn frowned, nodding furiously.

"You can take that as a 'hell yes'!" she said vehemently.

"I'll call you about it," Alanda said, turning to leave. "Nice to meet you," she said to Carmen on her way out.

It was then that Quinn remembered Carmen. Carmen, who had been standing there quietly, folding thick shoelaces during the entire time that Alanda had been in the store, hadn't made herself evident at all. It wasn't like Carmen to choose the background, so Quinn wondered if her co-worker had felt relegated to it.

Quinn waited though. She didn't start a conversation

just to see where Carmen's mind was, she just watched as Carmen's hands worked the thick shoelaces as if they were the most delicate things on earth. Finally, Carmen spoke.

"I didn't know you were working on an album," she said without looking up.

Quinn frowned, her lips pulling in a tight line across her face.

"I'm not, really," she said through an exhale. "I recorded a couple of songs I was doing to put together a demo, then I ran out of money."

Carmen nodded without looking up. There was a pause.

"Looks like you're gonna have all the money you need in a minute," Carmen said, her voice breaking a silence so heavy that it almost startled Quinn.

She chuckled.

"Guess so," she said.

"God bless you," Carmen said simply.

"Thanks."

"Can you do me a favor though?" Carmen asked innocently.

"What?"

For the first time since Alanda had come into the store, Carmen looked up and into Quinn's eyes.

"Can you find out for me if Bay-B has a big dick?"

She had just reached for the doorknob. She had been gambling. She knew it all along. She had been hoping against hope that time, or God, or whatever was at work would give her just one more day before starting her on a journey it would take her a week to complete. But it didn't. Time didn't. God didn't. Whatever didn't. She had just reached for the doorknob and now she'd have to walk back into her apartment, walk back into her bathroom, open a new box and put off all thoughts of sex with Caesar for until at least the following weekend. That is, unless she wanted to go out like Carmen. And she didn't wanna go out like that.

First sex was the worst. Well, at least it had always been for Quinn. You didn't know anything about the person. You didn't know about their rhythms or how they moved or anything. You didn't know what they wanted or what made them feel good. Worst of all, they didn't know anything about you. I mean, you knew the simple stuff. You knew he wanted his dick sucked and he knew you wanted your clit licked, but aside for the very vulgar and very generic, nobody knew anything. And there you'd be; two strangers staring at two strange naked bodies that came empty, without instruction manuals as to how to put them together, turn them on, and keep them running.

There had been exceptions to this rule, of course. Shortie had been an exception because she knew Shortie. The first time Shortie knelt between her legs had felt like the most natural thing in the world. It had been the extension that their love had been waiting for, the only road that their friendship hadn't taken. Then they took it and crashed. Life had been an exception too. But only because she hadn't expected anything from Life but that one night that she had found it in her somewhere to liberate herself and just totally bug the fuck out. In the case Life, their first sex had been the best. As time passed and expectations grew, the sex got worse and worse.

Quinn had hoped to get all the awkwardness of 'first sex' over with tonight. She had already decided that she liked Caesar enough to fuck him, now from the way that he fucked, she expected to decide whether she liked him enough to keep him. The truth was, she already liked Caesar more than she wanted to. That thing about having to leave to take care of his daughter had touched her more than she would have imagined something like that could have. She had seen so many 'baby-daddies' use their children as macking props, trying to play off the cuteness of their kids to get with her, that she had developed a built-in radar for that tactic.

"That's my little man!" Would be the part that was said, but "...And you can't imagine how much pussy he gets me!" would remain unsaid, yet still be heard by Quinn. But Caesar had seemed so genuinely concerned and privately concerned about not only the situation of his daughter, but his mother that was watching her, that Quinn had almost wanted to go with him to meet the whole lot. Not that she was thrilled about the idea of him having a daughter, she didn't have a child, but he had also probably not been involved in a disastrous marriage, which she had. Everybody had their own issues. And in the moments where she was either on Ex, weeded, or just inspired by what she considered to be God-given clarity, she found it hard to condemn anyone theirs when so many of hers were yet to be addressed.

"You look great," Caesar said, looking straight at her breasts that were, at present, uncontrollably huge and seemingly fighting to free themselves from the restrictive confines of her halter-top.

"Thanks," Quinn said half-heartedly. She knew she should have changed clothes. She didn't feel comfortable any more. She had only wanted to look sexy if there was a possibility for sex. Now she felt like an elaborate box and ribbon with no present inside. They took a seat.

It was Quinn's date. She made sure that that was established. She had called Caesar, she had invited him, and now she called the shots. Her idea of a good time was that they meet on lower Broadway in Manhattan and attend a show that she had heard about and had been dying to see. Some young woman had taken it upon herself to do a one-woman Sarah Vaughn revue, and as much as it offended Quinn, it intrigued her as well. Sarah Vaughn was her muse. Nobody understood Sarah or could fuck with her like Quinn could. Anybody else was just fooling themselves. So that was what Quinn had come out

to see. This young girl make a fool of herself. She did
intend to be objective, that's what she had brought Caesar
for. She didn't plan on trashing the show and then getting
him to agree, thereby making herself feel better. She was
gonna ask him seriously and honestly after the show was
over how he felt about it. If he liked it, fine. If he didn't, she
might just suck his dick.

Caesar was electric that night and Quinn knew what it
was that was all about. Yeah, he looked good. With his
frame, only the most hideous clothes could make him look
bad. Still, he had chosen a way to dress that fitted the
image of a man that she could see herself with. He was in
creams and browns and autumns (if that's a color.) He
looked good and groomed and slim and healthy in his
caramel-colored top coat, rich brown sweater and thick
brown corduroy pants. His shoes were a sweet toffee-
colored leather, and his skin, somewhere lost beneath all
that clothing, seemed to be yet another accessory that he
had put on to match.

For her part, Quinn had been all bundled, to the point
where when she took off her coat and the undercoat she
wore beneath it and her titties emerged, she could almost
watch the erection rise in Caesar's eyes. Her skirt was tight
and her ass even seemed to be jumping out a little, her high
boots making her look almost like a hooker. The kind of
hooker that a man would spend his last money on. All this
was serving to make him electric.

And he played the part well. Quinn had to credit him.
If he knew what he was doing, he was an expert, if he
didn't, his innocence was intoxicating. But the way he was

so totally and without interruption into her had made him irresistible to almost every other woman in the small but packed auditorium. All the girls seemed to be walking past, auditioning their wares for the man who couldn't take his eyes off her. Even the singer, when she finally did arrive on stage and began addressing the audience as she scanned the crowd, seemed struck by him. She spent a good portion of the night singing in his direction. But it was useless. He was with Quinn as assuredly as if he had been a disciple.

She was horny as fuck when the show was over. Not only was it the fact that all the female attention had been on Caesar, but the little playful exchanges that went on during the show had driven her crazy. He'd lean over and the back of his hand would gently brush against her nipple. She'd laugh at a joke that the performer made, her hand clawing deep into his upper thigh. If it had been just a little bit darker inside that tiny theatre, who knew what would have happened.

She kinda wished they had needed a cab to get back to her house. That way, they could have fooled around in the back seat and let somebody else do the driving. But Caesar drove. He drove a Toyota. And as the thoughts of ways to play in his lap ran into her mind and out, she decided against them, all in favor of waiting. She was so horny that if she did anything then, she would have made him have an accident.

They drove in silence, crossing the Brooklyn Bridge and headed back into her Fort Greene neighborhood with an anxiety towards each other that bordered on fear. There was nobody around now. Nobody to hide behind. Whatever was about to happen wouldn't be a performance, it would be for real and, after three years of bad, strange, and crazy relationships, the only thing in the world that Quinn didn't know if she was ready for was real life. So she breathed in deep when she got out of the car, leading Caesar by the hand as they walked towards the apartment.

"You have a nice place," he said, his voice breaking a little once she had finally opened the door.

"Thanks," she said. She knew his compliment was rote. Still, she would have never forgiven him had he not made it.

"What'd you think about that singer?" Quinn asked, trying her best to sound as if the question was rhetorical and that his fate for the night didn't rest with his answer.

"Well," Caesar said, taking a deep breath. "I thought she was alright. I mean, she didn't blow me away or anything."

Caesar wasn't even looking at Quinn really when he responded. He had taken a seat on the sofa. He was more or less looking around the apartment, her silhouette in his peripheral vision, not totally clear, but not completely out of view either. He was shocked by the appearance of her breasts, live, naked and up close. And they were huge. Huge. Bigger than anything he had ever seen. The nipples seemed like acorn sized antenna and the warm of their flesh as they bounced across his nose and mouth was almost suffocating. As bad as he wanted to suck them, he wanted to see them clearly. He wanted to marvel at them, to make sure they were real. But he couldn't see around them. Even the light had been asphyxiated.

He licked them, his tongue stoking the cleavage between, the tongue and mouth moving along the tremendous oval of the left one, towards that acorn of a nipple. When his mouth finally did arrive (and it seemed like it took forever) she let out a gasp as if the only thing she had ever been waiting for in the world was him to do just that. She grabbed them both herself from underneath, cupping them as if she was feeding them to him, knocking him backwards a little as the force of them being brought together was a little overwhelming. When he recovered, he was back at it, this time on the right nipple, her new gasp matching the last and as she moved the hand that held that breast, she used it to grab his own left hand, which had been resting on the small of her back. She placed his hand on her right breast, right in front of his mouth, and applied the pressure herself, making him squeeze. With her newly liberated hand, she reached for his belt. She flicked it open and unbuttoned his pants. Before reaching in, though, she slid her hand down along the front of his pants and touched a thing that distracted her a little. She didn't know what it was, but she knew what it wasn't. She knew what it couldn't be. There was no way it could be what she knew it wasn't. Maybe he travels with his own bottle of ketchup, she thought absently. Still, her hand's contact with it had been a sobering experience. She suddenly remembered Carmen and dry heaves in the bathroom at work earlier that afternoon.

"Excuse me for a second," she said, standing suddenly,

pulling the halter-top down and back over her breasts before turning and walking towards her bathroom.

"Okay," he said, a bit startled by all that had just happened, his eyes wide and his mouth hanging open. Quinn walked into her bathroom and turned on the light. She pulled up her skirt and down her pantyhose and panties. It was a bloodbath.

"Ugh," she moaned, her face contracting like a rancid smell had forced its way into her nostrils. There was just no way she could go through with this. Just no way...

"So you didn't do it," Carmen asked, her lips wrinkled as if disgusted.

"You should have seen it. It was crazy," Quinn pleaded.

"You didn't do it," Carmen repeated.

"I don't think it's ever been that heavy on the first day before," Quinn said.

"You didn't do it."

"What would he have thought of me?"

"You didn't do it."

"No."

Carmen sighed.

"You don't think that thing in his pants was his dick?" she asked after a pause.

"It couldn't have been," Quinn said, shaking her head. "Not unless he's a freak or something." Carmen shrugged. "Maybe he's a freak," she said, always the optimist.

Quinn shrugged.

"So what'd he, like, do?" Carmen asked. "How'd he take it?"

"He was cool," Quinn said. "He said he understood."
Then she laughed. "It was funny," she continued, looking
down and smiling. "He said he did it before with a girl on
her period. It was kinda like he was suggesting we
could..."

"See," Carmen cheered.

"But nah," Quinn negated. "I think I like him." And
with that quote remained an after-face as if the idea of her
actually liking somebody was as weird as a mayonnaise
sandwich to her.

Carmen shrugged.

"What if you like him and he's a freak," she asked, her
eyes flickering.

Quinn smiled wide.

"I think I'd be in love," she said.

"I think you are already," Carmen said.

"In love with who?" Bill asked, his presence on the
stairs a surprise and his voice an unwelcome intrusion.

"In love with you, Bill," Carmen mocked. "And that
big, cucumber dick I hear you got."

Bill looked surprised, then embarrassed, then rushed
back up the stairs.

"That'll keep him from coming for at least another five
minutes," Carmen said.

"More like thirty seconds," Quinn joked.

"You think you like this kid like that, though?" Carmen
asked.

"I dunno," Quinn began thoughtfully. "It's like... I've
seen so many things, you know? Been around so many
people, put up with so much bullshit. It's kinda hard to

start to trust people again. But this boy seems so pure. So innocent... If this is all just part of his game, then he's playing it like a mothafucka. But if any of it is true..."

"You found a good boy that you can corrupt," Carmen concluded with a seedy smile.

"Yeah," Quinn cheered slowly.

"That's beautiful," Carmen said evenly.

Joyce walked into the store. There was something about that girl, skyscraper tall as she was and with features and hair both wild and completely under control. Quinn hadn't seen her in a while and Carmen had never seen her at all. Hadn't heard about her, so when she saw that Quinn and the tall, peanut butter-colored girl were familiar, she went silent as she had when Alanda had come in a couple of days before.

"What's up, girl?" Quinn asked with a sort of happy incredulous tone that seemed to startle Joyce as she leaned back and her mouth parted a little.

"Hey Quinn," Joyce said in her broken, catty speaking voice.

"What brings you around?"

"I came to do some shopping for Phil," Joyce said. "That boy dresses like a farmer without crops."

Quinn squinted, trying to remember seeing that asshole: Phil Flarn in any clothing that stuck out in her memory.

"What does his wardrobe need?" Quinn asked, her concern seeming to surprise Joyce a little.

"A fireplace, a gallon of gas, and a match," Joyce said flatly.

"Damn," Carmen chuckled, her head down, her eyes on a group of wife-beater T-shirts she was folding. Quinn became aware of her co-worker.

"I'm sorry," she said to no one in particular. "Carmen, this is my friend Joyce. Joyce, this is Carmen."

The two women shook hands, each smiling at the pleasure of meeting another woman who meant them no harm.

"You looking for anything in particular?" Quinn asked.

"I'll know when I see it," Joyce said, as her eyes had already began roving the store, items to her liking attracting her towards them. While Joyce shopped, Carmen motioned Quinn towards her with her eyes.

"She's hot," Carmen whispered into Quinn's ear once Quinn had made her way over.

Quinn nodded. "She's a great singer too."

"Oh, so she's talented?" Carmen asked excitedly.

Quinn nodded.

"Think she'd do it with a girl?"

"I don't see why not," Quinn deadpanned. "She's doing it with an asshole."

"How is Phil?" Quinn called out across the store.

Joyce wrinkled her lips from where she was standing, near the denim cargo pants.

"Crazy," she said simply. "If we get married and have kids, you know what he wants to name the baby? Phillie," Joyce said as she grabbed a pair of pants and began walking towards Carmen and Quinn.

"What? Philly like Phil Flarn Jr or something?" Quinn asked.

"No," Joyce said.

"What? Philly like the city of Philadelphia?" Quinn asked.

"No," Joyce said, now standing right next to Carmen.

"Then Philly like what?"

"Phillie like the blunt."

"Oh my God…" Carmen moaned.

Quinn shook her head.

"What if you have a daughter?" she asked.

"Oh, Phillie's a unisex name," Joyce assured.

Quinn shook her head again.

"What if you have twins?" she asked.

"Phillie and White Owl."

"Poor babies," Carmen cried.

"Triplets?" Quinn asked.

"Phillie, White Owl, and Dutch Master."

"Are you really considering having this man's children?" Quinn asked through a wrinkled expression.

"I'm considering having this man committed," Joyce deadpanned.

Quinn shook her head.

"He's a great piano player, though," she sighed.

"Yeah, almost as good as he thinks," Joyce smirked, shaking her head. "But that's my baby…"

"You go, girl," Carmen cheered. "Stand by your crazy-ass man."

Joyce and Quinn laughed.

"She should talk," Quinn said to Joyce, motioning with her head towards Carmen. "Her man is crazier than Phil."

"You leave Steeze alone," Carmen defended.

"Steeze is your boyfriend?" Joyce asked. You could hear a pin drop. Carmen looked from Joyce to Quinn then back to Joyce. Joyce began to understand. "Oh, I don't know him like that," Joyce assured. "I did some background vocals on a song that this group on his label was putting out as a single."

"Oh," said Carmen and Quinn as a simultaneous sigh of relief.

"He's sweet," Joyce continued. "He was always talking about you. Talking about, 'My girlfriend's got the biggest ass!' Turn around," Joyce commanded. Carmen looked a little confused for a moment, then complied. "Yep," Joyce said, nodding her head while still looking at Carmen's ass. "He was right. He also said y'all got a little deal worked out."

"He told you about it?" Carmen asked, bordering on incredulous.

"Not like he wanted me to get down with it or anything," Joyce assured. "Just, like, to explain why you were the perfect girl for him and everything. He said you understood his temporary need for variety."

Carmen nodded unevenly.

"Does it make me look like a stupid girl or anything?" she asked, her face concerned.

"Not if you're getting yours too, which he said you were."

Carmen nodded again, this time more confidently.

"I'm gonna get some tonight," she cheered smiling. "This guy that Steeze knows. Shit, he just fucked this girl that I go to Journalism school with. I'ma hit this guy he used to breakdance with. I hope he's got a bigger dick than Steeze too."

"That's the spirit," Joyce agreed.

"Do you and Phil get down like that?" Carmen asked, curious.

"Please," Joyce said, waving her off. "If Phil even looked at another girl, I'd cut his eyes out."

"Now, that's the kind of relationship that I want," Quinn interrupted. "An eye for looking at an ass, a tooth for looking at a tush."

"Tush?" Carmen and Joyce asked simultaneously.

"It's an old expression," Quinn guaranteed.

"That's right, you are thirty-five," Carmen mocked as Joyce laughed and Quinn's face became stone.

"Thirty," she corrected.

"Same thing," Carmen and Joyce said simultaneously.

"Well, I see you guys have found new friends," Quinn mocked.

"Yeah, thanks Quinn," Joyce said brightly, leaning over and hugging Carmen, then beckoning with her hand for Quinn to come closer towards them. She begrudgingly came and was engulfed by a hug herself.

"You make good things happen," Joyce cheered. Quinn fought with and lost to an overwhelming desire to smile.

Joyce paid for the denim cargo pants and a sweater and walked out, her loping, left-to-right walking style her last remaining image.

"I like her," Carmen said, once she was out the door.

"It's hard not to," Quinn said, shaking her head.

"So you think you really might fall in love with this kid,

huh?"

Quinn lay on her bed, the index finger of her right hand intertwining with her pubic hair as she thought. Carmen's last question had never really left her mind. Might she fall in love with Caesar? Shit, had she been in love before? Who knew? How could you tell? Certainly, every time love was over, I mean, really over, the only healthy thing to do was to deny that you had ever been in love at all. She hadn't loved Cedric, but she had married him. She hadn't loved Life, but she had stayed with him during one of the most trying years of her existence. She hadn't loved Shortie... well, she hadn't loved Shortie like that... Well, okay, maybe it was cool to admit that she had been in love with Shortie. Maybe, because it was less threatening. Maybe because she wasn't supposed to love Shortie and the possibility of loving Shortie didn't present her with anything as far as the future was concerned, made actually loving Shortie that much easier. It was just too dangerous to love men. They might do anything.

Shortie might have left at any time but, sure, Shortie was supposed to. They had both known when they got into the relationship that it would end eventually. Or at least, that it would change. Both women wanted children. Quinn wanted a man. And Shortie, as much as she might have protested, wouldn't have been too angry if she had ended up with a man herself. Shit, she ended up with something that really strongly resembled a man. It had a dick and all. It might have even had balls, it was just that Shortie controlled them. But Quinn didn't want the kind of man that Shortie had. And when she thought about that man, her man, she remembered a time when he had been so clear that if he just came walking along one day right up on the street, she would have snatched him up because she would have recognized him from all the times she had seen him in her thoughts.

Her hand moved lower…

She would indulge the girls when they gathered in circles after jumping rope and hopscotch.

"Michael Jackson," she'd say. He was a cutie back in them days. He had that big ass afro and he could dance. He could sing too, fuck what everybody tried to say. And she was defensive of him. Nobody could talk about Michael. She hated New Edition, at first. They were trying to be like Michael and his brothers. The only benefit to them and the one that would eventually win her over was the fact that they were closer to her age. The likelihood of actually marrying one of them was a lot greater than it was of marrying Michael, who would almost certainly have taken a bride by the time that she was of marrying age. But even Michael was just an answer for the girls. Her man, well, the man she had in mind would be better than Michael was. Sure, he'd be able to sing and dance as well as Michael, but he'd have muscles too. And he'd be a good basketball player. And a good cook. And he'd be rich. He'd sort of be a combination Michael/Dr J/that guy with the bald spot and the funny sideburns from the Black Enterprise magazines that her father read/her father too, cause she loved her father. And he could cook.

Quinn didn't remember exactly when the mathematics

of what her mother and father were actually doing when she would watch them during their Al Green sofa theatrics kicked in. Whatever it was, it didn't seem enjoyable. Not for her father at least. His face would always be wrinkled in the most tortured distortions while her mother just laughed and drank. Quinn had figured that it was something that her father did just to appease her mother and couldn't understand why even as a really little girl, so many of the boys, especially the older ones, seemed willing to appease her the same way. Then it clicked.

Her hand moved lower…

The first guy that did her right really opened up a door for her. He was this dude in college with a really beautiful dick. But it wasn't just his dick, she understood only much later. It was the fact that he talked during sex. Like he was narrating the experience to her during the act. The whole thing was like a documentary and, as much as she was into information at the time, that aspect of it really turned her on. Unfortunately, she got tired of seeing the same show over and over again. And she decided to start seeing others, even if they weren't as good.

Her hand moved lower…

But she had been in love before. And that thought nearly froze her hand. She knew she was in love when she was in love. She always denied it to herself so heavily. She always looked at it as an obstacle, as opposed to a condition. She always sought to liberate herself from it, as opposed to immersing herself in it. She had always blamed herself for falling, like she was a victim of a crime precaution could have prevented. It was apathy. This love thing swallowing her whole from all sides, clouding all her decisions and making her feel trapped, always trapped by itself and not the person she was supposed to be feeling it for. Cedric could come or go but her love for him was a motha. Life could come or go, but her love... it would be there. Shortie was supposed to be able to come or go, but when she left, something went with her. Something even more frustrating than she could have imagined because she had always known Shortie would go. Had always expected Shortie to go. Had planned for it. Had hoped for it, actually. Had done everything but induce it. And then it happened: without her notification.

She was fucking herself now. Angrily. For Shortie... Cause Shortie must have hated her to do her like that. She was bringing herself there alone. Alone seemed to be the only way she'd get anywhere. Her mind wasn't with her. She was working on pure emotion now. The skin of herself pulled back, the tip of the thing exposed to the point where even the air was her seducer. She was on her way...

Then Caesar came along and she slowed. As if her mind was working against her now, bringing Caesar into the view she had behind closed eyes. Caesar smiling, telling her that the singer they'd seen was just "Okay." Quinn was smiling now too, her finger moving slower and slower, the sensation however, strangely growing. Then Carmen joined Caesar and, for some reason, things became even better. The top of her palm was touching the thing now as her fingers roved and explored. Caesar and Carmen. She could love them both. The thought parted her lips.

It wasn't as if it had ever made sense, this love and sex

thing. She had loved Cedric, but hated fucking him, loved
Life long after she stopped loving to fuck him, loved
Shortie… It was as if something in her mind had told her
not to even try to associate love with good dick, good
pussy or whatever was good that made one cum. Not to
even try it. If you have your cake, then you eat it, it's gone,
so you have to choose one or the other. But maybe with
Caesar, if that thing in his pocket hadn't been a ketchup
bottle… or maybe with Carmen if that ass in the flesh was
that ass in her dreams…

And she would love them both too: well. She would
love them with everything she had inside. And that's
where her love had always been: inside. She had tried to
bring it out, failing spectacularly, giving only tokens of
love and being rewarded with rides not unlike a subway.
Love had always been a reward when given from her, she
had loved Cedric for marrying her, she had loved Life for
staying with her, she had loved Shortie for loving her. It
would be a wondrous thing just to love simply because
that was how she felt and nothing else mattered. She
would tell them she loved them, then instead of standing
aside as she always had, sure that the love would run, she
would stand still and watch them because it didn't matter
really what they did next. They could do whatever they
wanted. She would love them still.

The thing was now massive, throbbing and eager…

Love. It was funny, but love had never made her cum.
Love had made her sad. Love had frustrated her and
confused her, beat her and held her unmercifully against
her will. Love had tormented and teased her, appearing for

a moment as a possibility, only to reveal itself much later to be something else. But this time she would love first. Not sitting back waiting as she always had for the words to come from the mouth of another so she could plan a counter-attack based on a strategy she believed the situation needed. This time she would love without expectation, because all she expected was to love. And who could expect anything better than that?

The floor was scarred like the back of a slave the next morning when Quinn awoke. The tire marks her bed had left had startled her until she remembered how hard she had shook the night before. Had she cum hard? She must have. She couldn't remember anything else. She had passed away into a dead sleep so sound that not only had she slept through the alarm clock, but also when she picked up her phone on her nightstand to call Bill and tell him that she was running late, there were four new messages on her voicemail. The first one was from Alanda.

"Get ready," was all her voice said before the call disconnected.

The next was from Life.

"Just wonderin' what you was doin', what you was up to, how you been..." 'Can I come by soon and get some pussy?' was the part that remained unrecorded.

The next was from Bill.

"You fired!" he screamed. "Now get your ass to work." The last was from Caesar.

"I been thinking about you way too much lately," he said softly. "What you been thinking about?"

I love you," she said. Carmen stood, looking at her from the distance, her face more confused than concerned.

"What'd you say?" she asked, as if her hearing had gone.

"I said, I love you," Quinn said simply again.

Carmen closed her eyes tight and shook her head.

"That's what you had to tell me?" she asked when she opened her eyes again. Quinn nodded. Carmen approached. She wrapped her arms around the small of Quinn's back, kissed her on the cheek and whispered, "Hold me" in her ear.

Quinn uneasily wrapped her arms around Carmen's back.

"Grab my ass," Carmen instructed. Quinn followed instructions.

It was unlike anything that Quinn had ever felt. It seemed impossible, so big, so round, so soft and so firm. She wanted to see it to smell it to kiss it to taste it to rub her face along the outside of it to be one with it. How could one woman possess something so astonishing? Carmen kissed her, pulling her head away from the side of Quinn's face where it had been and moving it back before making eye contact with Quinn and moving in. Their tongues met first. Carmen sucked her tongue so tightly that Quinn felt as if the life was being pulled out of her through her lover's mouth. She reached a hand inside the front of Carmen's pants. Then they heard a crash.

"Shit," Quinn hissed, as Carmen began to giggle and Quinn began to race upstairs.

"Bill," she screamed, before she had even reached the door. She pulled the key from her front pocket and unlocked it. Bill was there, on the floor, trapped beneath his lamp and poking out from his pants.

"What was that?" he asked, in a completely normal speaking voice that surprised Quinn. She stammered.

"Um... Carmen's got a role in an independent film," she said after a moment. "There's a lesbian scene in it. She asked me if I'd rehearse with her."

Bill motioned with his head for Quinn to help him. She began lifting the lamp and uncoiling the wiring.

"If that was any indication of what she's got," Bill began, returning to his feet and still sticking out of his pants, "the girl's a star. You too, Quinn. I would have sworn to God that kiss was authentic."

Quinn smiled an uneasy smile but noticed that Bill wasn't paying any attention to her face. He was too busy tucking himself back into his pants.

"Thanks," Quinn said, looking between where Bill's hands had been and his face. He shrugged unevenly, smiling. Quinn began walking out.

"Oh Quinn..." Bill called behind her. "I don't know if it'll mean anything," he began, "but I was fantasizing about you too that time."

Quinn shook her head, walked out of the office and closed the door. She paused for a moment outside Bill's door. She didn't want Carmen to see her smiling. It just didn't make sense. There would have been no way in the world, she realized, that she would have been able to explain to anybody why she had been happy to be included in some pervert's sexual fantasy. But she was.

The next few days were hard. Both Carmen and Quinn were more familiar with each other's rhythms than they would have ever allowed themselves to imagine. Carmen always came in first and left first. She also always took lunch at twelve. Exactly twelve. Quinn always lunched at one. She would come in dragging and leave the same way. Now that they were both in love and aware that they were constantly being watched, the glaring differences in the scheduling became salted open sores. There was just no way that they could connect with each other without it seeming staged. There was no way that they could come in together or leave together or take lunch together without something seeming 'funny'. And the last thing that either wanted, especially as far as Bill was concerned, was for anything to seem 'funny'. So they stole glances and smiles, whispered and talked out of the sides of their mouths.

It seemed so amazing to Quinn, after that first day, that she didn't know anything more about Carmen than she had learned in the first week of working with her. She didn't know her home phone number, she didn't know exactly where she lived, she didn't know where she partied and she didn't wanna ask. She figured that she had

made the first advance and figured that if Carmen wanted
her, she would reciprocate. She would be patient. So for the
rest of the week, they played cat and mouse. Quinn
sneaking a pinch of that mountain of an ass whenever it
was in close enough proximity, Carmen with her hands in
the most awkward of positions to rub along the ovals of
Quinn's pendulous breasts whenever a chance encounter
found them in the same section of the store. Each would go
into the bathroom and stay for eternities, fully aware of
what the other was doing. Neither could wait for Bill to
start filming another movie which would keep him out of
the office for weeks on end.

"Mothafuckin' Phil Flarn," came the voice.

Oh my God, Quinn thought. The asshole announces
himself. Quinn's week of store love with Carmen had been
so all-encompassing that she had almost totally forgotten
about the outside world. Almost. But when the voice went
up as the door flew open and the asshole came in, she
knew that her paradise had been lost and it was time to get
back to reality.

"What's up, girlfriend?" the drummer said, one step
behind that asshole: Phil Flarn, who had already traveled
all the way across the store and now stood directly before
her.

"Hey Trent," Quinn said to the drummer. "What do you
want, Phil?"

Phil Flarn shook his head.

"It's bad to 'want'," he said simply. "It makes it seem
like you're not pleased with the job that God's already
done for you. It's better just to be thankful for what you've

got and eventually good things comes to pass."

"What?" Quinn asked.. That sounded too much like something Life would say.

"This mothafuckin' shirt that Joyce bought is too small," Phil Flarn said.

"Too small," the drummer said, echoing.

"Were you with him when he tried it on, Trent?" Quinn asked with a sly smile.

"Hell, yeah," the drummer hissed.

"He liked me in it," Phil Flarn said. "The fuckin' homo."

"Better than what you are," the drummer said so hotly that if Quinn didn't know him, didn't know that asshole: Phil Flarn and didn't know that this was a game that they always played, she might have thought that he was really becoming angry.

"What am I?" Phil Flarn asked with interest.

"A homo in denial," the drummer said.

"How's that better?" Phil Flarn said.

"Cause I'm being true to myself."

"I know. You're being a true homo. Now me, I may be a homo in denial, I mean, a dick might cross my mind every so often, but I don't wanna suck it, I don't wanna ride it. You do… And do!"

The drummer burst out laughing. Followed by Carmen who'd had her head down in the front of the store, folding some basketball shorts. Phil Flarn and the drummer looked towards her, before turning back to Quinn who was trying to cover up the laughter on her own face.

"Phil, I didn't know you were a homo in denial," Quinn

said mocking.

Phil Flarn shrugged unevenly.

"Sure," he said simply. "I deny everything. Can you get me a bigger shirt?"

Quinn smirked and began looking around on the table with the sweatshirts for one that matched the pattern of the one Phil Flarn was holding in his hands, but in a larger size.

"What size do you need?" she asked, as she began rifling through.

"You got double-x?" he asked.

She turned to him with an incredulous look.

"How big are you?" she asked through wrinkled lips.

"You think I'ma answer that question with this guy around?" Phil Flarn said, motioning with his head to a chuckling drummer.

"He doesn't wanna disappoint me," the drummer said, still laughing.

"Nah, but seriously Phil," Quinn began again. "Why do you need a double extra large?"

"That's the size I wear," Phil said evenly.

Quinn shrugged and resumed her search. Finding a sweatshirt in the size he requested she pulled it out of the stack and tossed it to Phil Flarn. Phil Flarn unfolded it in his hands before him, holding it up in front of his face. He smiled broadly.

"That's what I'm talking about," he said, as proud as a new father. "I don't need to fill out any forms or anything do I?" he asked of Quinn. "I can just bounce, right?"

Quinn nodded. Phil Flarn nodded in return.

"Good lookin' Quinn," he said, stuffing the sweatshirt in the bag he had been carrying the other one in.

"You two sure are buddy-buddy," Quinn couldn't resist teasing.

Phil Flarn looked confused.

"Who?" he asked. "Me and Homo Erectus here?"

Carmen cackled a surprising laugh again as Quinn, Phil Flarn and the drummer turned to face her.

"Yeah," Quinn said once Phil Flarn and the drummer had turned back towards her. "What's up Phil? You two-timing Joyce with Trent here?"

Phil Flarn shook his head.

"He doesn't like me like that," he said evenly. "If he did, I wouldn't hang with him."

"Why?" Quinn asked, frowning.

"What am I gonna hang with a man that's sexually attracted to me for?" Phil Flarn asked. "So I can get drunk one night and claim shit was an accident? Hell no! That's some shit women do. Hang with other girls they wanna fuck." He paused to shake his head. "You probably wanna hit off honey over there," he continued, motioning with his head towards Carmen. When he saw the look on Quinn's face though, he instantly felt uncomfortable. Like perhaps he had gone too far.

"Gotta go," he said quickly. "Good lookin' like I said. And hey, give my nigga a call. I think he loves you. *So what is he so afraid of…?*" Phil sang as he whirled and headed towards the door.

"How'd you know I wasn't attracted to you?" the drummer asked as he turned and followed Phil Flarn.

"Nigga, I know when a man wanna fuck me," Phil Flarn yelled as he opened the door and headed out. "It's too bad you don't too cause if I was a fag, you'd be the kind of nigga I wanted to get with. All little and shit. I could just see myself smacking that ass as I was fucking you from behind…"

Once the door had closed and Phil Flarn and the drummer were completely gone, Carmen walked across the store towards Quinn.

"That was Joyce's boyfriend?"

Quinn looked at her and nodded but her mind was clearly elsewhere.

"He's crazy," Carmen continued, aware that something was troubling her friend.

Quinn shrugged unevenly. Carmen touched Quinn's right shoulder with her own right hand twice, then turned and walked away.

Phil Flarn was an asshole, that much was certain. But strangely, Quinn wasn't mad at Phil Flarn right then. She didn't feel anything at all for him. All he was doing was being himself. It was herself that she had a problem with, she thought, as she glanced across the room and saw the beauty of a back-at-work Carmen folding shirts against the sunlight that was breaking through the front window of the store. She didn't want to address what she felt, but she knew what it was. It was shame. She was ashamed about how she felt about Carmen. Like there was something wrong with it. And if she felt that there was something wrong with it, then there was something wrong with it. It was a vicious circle. How she envied the drummer right then. Phil Flarn could call him a 'faggot' like the word was the only one he knew and if it was funny, the drummer laughed, if it wasn't the drummer ignored it. It seemed to her that the drummer had accepted it. His being a 'faggot'. Even if that wasn't the way he felt about himself or the word he would have chosen to define himself, he seemed to realize that this was the way the world saw him. And since the majority of the world could only deal in simple concepts, it was useless to try to broaden the world's perspectives. It was best to simply just be that 'faggot' for those limited enough to only see him as that. And for those with enough range to see him as a man, as the drummer, as Trent, he'd be a man, the drummer, Trent. Who really had time to worry about everyone else?

But Quinn wasn't there yet. She also wasn't gay. She wasn't even sure if she was bisexual. She just knew that she had been attracted to a couple of women. Shortie had been one of them. Carmen was the other. And it had gone beyond attraction with each of them. She actually loved them both. Maybe that was what had made the attraction so viable. She had loved Shortie, so sex with her seemed like just another something to be shared between them. Now she loved Carmen. And, like with Shortie, it wasn't that she wanted to spend the rest of her life in a sexual relationship with Carmen, but she did want to share something with her. Something physical. As boyish as it sounded, she just had to have that ass.

But that asshole: Phil Flarn, in his infinite ability to make everything seem shameful, had added another issue to Quinn's list of concerns: Caesar. Where did he fit in on her list of desires and sexual urges? Would he understand? Would he need to have it explained? Was it better to just do what she felt she needed to do and offer no explanation or details? Men were such cowards, this she knew. Anything they hadn't, wouldn't, or couldn't do they expected to be off-limits to the women they dealt with. It was a wonder that they 'allowed' women to give birth.

But Caesar had shown flashes of difference. He seemed like he might be that one in a thousand of men that wouldn't be afraid or intimidated by a woman's honest desires. She pictured telling him face to face, "I just wanna eat her ass," and him shrugging unevenly, understanding. That would be beautiful. She'd love him for a lifetime.

But then the flip side of that could potentially be just as disturbing. I mean, like, what after she just explained her forbidden desires to Caesar, he explained some of his to her? What if he was like, "And I just want the drummer to lotion up my backside and…"

Ugh, Quinn shuddered. She knew she was using a double standard, but she felt entitled. She wanted to be the only faggot in her relationship with a man. Was that too much to ask?

"Carmen," she called out, looking up from her thoughts across the room to her friend. Carmen looked up. "Love you," she cheered.

"Love you too," Carmen said in return as Bill, from his office, had to pause and consider the meaning of all this talk as he knelt by his two-way office glass.

S hortie was pregnant. The news hit Quinn like a blow. That dyke bitch was gonna have a baby. The luck some people had. She lived her fantasy dyke life, then when it was time, found a faggot, made him a man, and got him to get her pregnant. She'd have him where she wanted him too. And, because of this, be able to prove at any time she needed or at any time she wanted that she didn't love him. If she loved him, would she treat him the way she did? Would she talk to him the way she did? Of course she would. She'd love him 'cause he'd let her talk to him and treat him like that. She needed to and he'd let her.

Quinn knew from the beginning that she couldn't be what Shortie wanted. Shortie wanted to dominate. And what probably turned Shortie on the most about Quinn was the fact that she couldn't, and wouldn't have ever been able to dominate Quinn. So she fucked her. At least she'd have that.

How had she dominated all those men? The women, Quinn could understand. Shortie was sexy as hell. Everybody was attracted to sexiness. Sexiness was coed. But the thugs and hardrocks Shortie would leave crying like bitches were enigmatic resolutions. How did that happen? Quinn had known all along. Shortie watched men. She studied them. She learned what fucked with them whether it be dick size or intellect. If a man didn't like his money or his mama, Shortie could tell. And Shortie would use it.

Poor boys were set in perpetual motion trying to prove her wrong. Their dicks would grow or they'd get smarter or they'd get their money together or they'd get their mama together. But it would never be enough. It would never impress Shortie. Even if it did. Quinn would shake her head at the poor souls, glad that she wasn't a boy and didn't have to put up with any of Shortie's bullshit. She'd have shown Shortie if she was a boy. She'd have said, "Bitch, I don't have to impress you," at the first one of Shortie's criticisms or snide remarks. That would have set her straight. Too bad she wasn't a boy…

And that night had been such a set-up on both parts. She had decided in her mind long before that night that she was gonna fuck Shortie. She was gonna use Cedric as an excuse. She let herself get too drunk, but she knew what she was doing. Then she was gonna give Shortie the opportunity they'd both been waiting for. She hoped Shortie had the balls for it.

Then Shortie got what she wanted. It really didn't bother Quinn. What bothered her was that Shortie had gotten what she wanted before she had. It would have been wonderful if they had both gotten what they wanted simultaneously, but if somebody had to be left waiting, she'd have preferred it to be Shortie. She didn't want to feel like the pressure was on, but it was. Shortie was pregnant now. Her life was going where she wanted it to go. Quinn would have to do something soon. She'd either have to come up with the perfect man, a baby, or start singing for real. Hopefully all three. Soon.

Not that Caesar was feeling any pressure. He never felt pressure. He could walk between the raindrops. He'd get wet if he wanted to. And Quinn kinda made him wanna get wet. He'd have torn that shit up if she'd have given it to him that night. Period or not. He didn't want her to think he was nasty though, so... Funny thing was, he wondered if she didn't want him to think she was nasty. He wouldn't have minded. But there was something to be said for patience. Something. He didn't know what it was. He wanted all of his right now. He guessed he'd get it when he got it. And when he did...

But he liked Quinn as a chick, as a woman, even. She was cool. She had something to say. He didn't know if he agreed with it or not. He just knew he liked to hear it. He liked her company and liked watching the world unfold through her eyes. He didn't know how long he would keep on liking it, but he liked liking it right then. He believed that he might like it a while. He just wanted to fuck her and do what ever was necessary to continue.

So he had something romantic planned. Fruits and vegetables. A smörgåsbord of delights. He'd even spray some whipped cream on her ass. Yeah... that was it.

Caesar zipped up and washed up. That was a good one. His head was clear now. He could think. What would he do next in his wonderful world of opportunity, now that he had this Quinn situation handled?

"Quinn!" She turned and looked at the next chick. It was funny hearing her name shouted on the subway platform. She wasn't surprised that it was Shortie.

"What's up, girl," Quinn shouted, smiling like her face was going to break, and diving into a hug across a great distance. Shortie caught her.

"What's been up?" Shortie asked.

Dumb question, Quinn thought.

"Life," she said, shrugging as if she couldn't think of anything else.

"Heard you got a new man," Shortie sneered.

Quinn flinched.

"Who could have told you that?" she asked, looking around suspiciously.

"Just heard," Shortie said.

"Nah, I just play with myself a lot now, basically," Quinn sneered herself finally. "How's the dick you're getting?"

Shortie felt burned.

"Damn," she said, leaning away like there had been heat coming off Quinn's words.

"Why you worried about who I'm fucking?"

Shortie squinted, but ended up shrugging. "I was just happy for you," she said simply.

"Fucking would make me happy?" Quinn asked.

"It does for me," Shortie shrugged.

Quinn laughed. Shortie did too. But they were mad at each other so they didn't share the laugh.

"Where are you going?" Shortie asked.

Quinn paused to speak. She was going to meet Caesar.

"Just chilling," she said.

"You going someplace by yourself?" Shortie asked, concerned.

"Yeah," Quinn said unevenly.

Shortie shrugged and wrinkled her face.

"Well, have fun," she mock cheered.

Quinn quickly nodded her away. The train came and she got on and sat down as it took off. But she couldn't get that uneven look off her face.

"So you told her I had a boyfriend?" she asked.

Carmen nodded. She seemed a little concerned, but still convinced. She had done the right thing.

"Why?" Quinn continued.

"Well, she came in about a week ago," Carmen began. "It was way before you usually come in. Anyway, she's got this dude with her. This dredlocked, funny-looking dude."

Quinn nodded with disgust.

"And she's waving him around like he's a ring," Carmen continued. "And she's all, like, 'Well tell her Shortie and what's-his-face dropped by and we were just in the neighborhood and we wanted to check her out and see what was going on…' Stuff like that. So I said, 'Quinn's doing great. She got a new man and all. Won't bring him by the store and won't let me check him out…' I left it at that. I didn't overdo it."

Quinn didn't know how to feel. Carmen had done what a friend would have done. They looked at each other.

"Thanks," Quinn found a way to say.

"You're welcome," Carmen said with pep. "So what happened last night?"

She had finally found a way to schedule something with Caesar. It had taken about two weeks. It was this wine and cheese affair being given by these girls in Harlem that wanted Quinn to sing in a group with them. She did want an excuse to see Caesar though, so she agreed to the affair. He picked her up impossibly in Brooklyn and drove. He sat politely through talk that centered around Quinn being part of a female R&B group. She left unconvinced. But Caesar drove her home, parked out front, came inside and stripped her down. It had all happened so quickly. Everything was out, exposed, and eager. Then the phone rang.

"You ready," Alanda asked on the line.

"Hell, yeah!" Quinn said, surveying Caesar's naked body.

"Do you know who this is?" Alanda asked, perturbed.

"No," Quinn said, perturbed.

"It's Alanda, it's time to do the Bay-B song."

"Now?" Quinn demanded.

"Now," Alanda said before hanging up.

Seventy-five thousand dollars was a mothafucker. Caesar understood as he put on his pants.

"You got something to do tonight?" she asked, as politely as she felt it.

He paused with his pants up, and shook his head.

"Could you wait for me then?" she asked. He seemed confused. "For a while," she added. And he shrugged unevenly, turned on the television and sat down.

Of course, Bay-B wasn't at the studio when she got there. He was home in bed. Alanda hadn't called him yet. She decided to call him when Quinn got there. So Quinn had to wait for him.

"I apologize for Alanda," the smooth talking MC said when he strolled into the studio. "She has a history of mental cruelty."

Quinn laughed, overcome with humor and charisma. As nervous as she was, she delivered the goods in one take.

"What you getting ready to get into?" Bay-B asked on her way out.

"Just headed home," she said with a smile as she got in the cab.

Caesar was gone when she got there.

"Damn," Carmen said, after hearing about Quinn's night. She shook her head.

Quinn looked exhausted from simply reliving the tale.

"So since you did see Caesar naked this time," Carmen began again, "Is his dick really as big as a ketchup bottle?"

Quinn had wondered if it would be awkward. This being the next time that she saw Caesar after he had left that night. Carmen had suggested it. She and Steeze were going out, getting away from people. They did that on occasion by disappearing: among the white people. If white people were good for one thing, Quinn had always theorized, it was that they didn't care about you. You could be amongst them and as long as you weren't dealing with them, looking at them or talking to them, they weren't dealing with, looking at or talking to you. This was comforting to Quinn sometimes when her people seemed a bit too oppressive or interested. When the bars she liked or the clubs she would have ordinarily frequented seemed too limited. But even escaping among the whites had its limitations. Nobody cared about you. And it was a rare mood indeed that found Quinn eager for a situation where nobody cared about her.

Caesar walked in on time after Quinn, Carmen and Steeze had already been seated. It was a small bar in midtown that served, among other things, buffalo wings and potato skins. Steeze was all for the All-American shit. He had ordered the wings, the skins and was starting on his second jug of Budweiser when the other male of the evening arrived. He reached up to touch fists with Caesar who he remembered from their mixtape talks. He immediately looked over to Carmen who he remembered offering herself to Caesar. He shrugged.

"What's up, man?" Caesar asked of Steeze.

"Nice to see you again," he said with a smile to Carmen.

"Hey Ms Quinn," he offered to the first lady.

Quinn nodded to him appreciatively.

Caesar looked around. He had never been too big on white people himself, always finding himself suspicious of them and their tendency to think they were right. He had always found their logic inconclusive at best, just plain faulty at worst, and had figured that an ideal world would be one in which race relations were restricted to respectful unspoken passes in the street. But these white people didn't seem to be like the ones he had known all his life in New London. The ones that had irritated him in high school and tormented him with their ineptitude at work. These white people were drunk, trying to get some pussy, and in their own worlds. It was the only time that he had felt a sense of kinship with them.

"You drinkin'?" Steeze asked, as Caesar's hip nudged into place besides Quinn's on the sofa-chair.

"You pourin'?" Caesar asked, extending a plastic cup.

Steeze tilted the mug of beer and poured.

"Who's idea was this place?" Caesar asked after nodding and mumbling his 'thanks' to Steeze.

"Steeze picked it," Carmen rushed to say.

Quinn eyed her with a smirk. So proud of her man, Quinn thought, with what might have been contempt if she hadn't been so proud of Caesar right then. He looked good. She didn't think he was the type of dude that could do the color black, being that he was so brown-colored and his eyes were almost green, but in he came: black shirt, black slacks, black shoes. That thick gold thing on his neck was flashing like he was new money. And the contents of his pants had been a hot issue of debate before his arrival, with even Steeze making inquiries. Then the way he called her 'Ms Quinn…' Quinn wanted to strip him down right there. She adjusted her halter-top instead.

Carmen looked quickly from Quinn's huge shaking breasts to Steeze's face and then down to his lap. She slapped down under the table, connecting with something that sounded like flesh.

"Stop that!" she warned as Steeze pulled his hand out above the table and tried to wave off the effects of the slap. Carmen looked back at Quinn. "You should have seen what he was doing," she said to her friend angrily. "When you adjusted your top, he grabbed his dick!"

Quinn laughed. Uncomfortable at first, but was relieved to be able to laugh heartily when Caesar joined her. She thought he might have been offended by such bawdiness.

"Caesar, have you seen them shits yet?" Steeze asked, now ready for more laughs.

Caesar nodded.

"They crazy?" he shook his head, but in a 'you-just-don't-know' type way.

"That's what I thought," Steeze said, nodding though fantasizing.

"Quinn," Carmen demanded angrily. "Make them stop."

Quinn was smiling from ear to ear.

"Oh, but don't sleep on my baby, though," Steeze said, quickly becoming serious. "She got all the ass a nigga needs. Her ass is so big I make her kneel in the passenger's seat of my ride cause I can't shift gears if she's sitting down next to me."

After a great deal of thought, both Quinn and Caesar got the joke and laughed.

Quinn was getting a little horny though. She thought of the most recent night she and Caesar had been together and how they had both been so direct. The time before must have done something to them because they both moved this time like everything had been planned. Her breasts had nearly jumped out of her bra. Her nipples were about as hard and big as a 4-carat diamond. Caesar had unzipped before doing anything else, even taking off his shirt. It was funny how the lighting was in the apartment because when she looked for it, and it was the first thing she looked for, it looked funny, like it was there, but it couldn't be there. Like it had to be a mistake. Like a shadow or something must have been making it seem different from what it was, what it must have been. That's why she couldn't wait to get it inside her. She couldn't believe what she was seeing. Then Alanda called.

Now he sat there beside her. She wanted to be angry with him. She wanted to be angry with him for leaving. She wanted to act like she was so outraged that he had decided that he couldn't wait for her that she never wanted to see him again. The truth was, the fact that he wasn't there just made her want him more. If he had been there, she didn't know how she would have felt about him. She didn't know if she would have still respected him. If she could have made him wait this time, she could keep him waiting. But he was gone. Him and whatever that thing was he held between his legs.

He had called the next day to make sure she had gotten in safe. She made sure that she sounded a little angry over the phone. He seemed to shrug off her sound.

"How was it?" he had asked.

"Cool," she said. "Bay-B was cool. Everything was cool."

"Bay-B," Caesar said, and Quinn couldn't picture him nodding through the phone. "That guy's a good MC."

"One of the best," Quinn cheered.

"Was it worth it?"

That question had hung there. That was why she couldn't hate him. She had, in fact, left him. He was ready and she put him on pause. What he had done had just been a response. She had initiated the hurt. Of course, he shouldn't have been hurt, she realized. He should have understood. Should have, because well she knew that some men didn't seem to understand anything.

I want to fuck you, but this will be my only chance to get this money

She would have explained it if she had been fluent in boy-talk. But she could only speak as she wanted to be spoken to and as such said, "I gotta go. I gotta sing on this song. I promised." Then she walked out of the door that night leaving him shirtless and waiting. And now she was seventy-five thousand dollars richer.

"Yeah," she said over the phone. "It was worth it. But do you know what my next priority is?"

They met up with Steeze and Carmen to get drunk for cheap amongst the white people in midtown. After Caesar had charmed them as Quinn was growing to imagine that he charmed everybody, the foursome headed off into the night.

It was a Tuesday and, as such, the bar called The Wooden Indian was going on. It was a spot that served the twentysomething, 'still-in-the-singles game, but looking a little ridiculous in clothes much more suitable for a younger adult' crowd. Steeze led the charge. He took over the dance floor doing splits and other moves so complicated that they looked like they had been choreographed by Einstein. He had been the man at the door, shaking hands and hugging onlookers, blowing, pecking, and receiving kisses. It was clearly his type of place.

Caesar had come in on a quieter agenda. He whisked Quinn away past the dreds and the hardheads, past the hoochies and pigeons, pass the ballers, players, hustlers, pimps, hoes, bitches, and black people in attendance. He got her in a corner by herself, then he wrapped a hand around her back and, in contradiction to the music that was playing, began to slow dance with her. His thigh was high into her crotch. The sensation sent a chill through her.

"You think you know my body well enough to toy with it?" she asked, her face bordering on a smile.

Caesar shook his head. He ran his hand along the small of her waist, from right under her armpit to the crest of her hip.

"I just like the landscape," he said, as he looked at the space between her extended arm and body like a surveyor.

"You're appraising me?" she asked, her top row of teeth playing a tune across her lip.

He nodded.

"Thinking about moving in," he said simply. In one swift movement, her hand was between his legs.

"I don't know if I want your type in here," she said, looking him in the eye until she said the word 'here'. When she said that, her eyes ran the length of her own body. "You might make too much noise," she continued.

"Or make you make too much," Caesar said as calmly as he could, considering the fact that a woman was holding him by the nuts. He began to stiffen in her hand. She quickly moved her hand away and began to look around.

"What's wrong?" he asked, smiling slyly.

"I don't want that thing to get hard and then have everybody in here looking at you," she said quickly.

"Don't know if you want me to move in, but don't want me looking at other available real estate?" he mocked.

Quinn rested her hands on her hips.

"Go ahead," she said defiantly. "Show me the money. Pull it out. See if I care. You'll probably grab the attention of more faggots than females. It's probably what you want anyway. Anybody that hangs out with Phil Flarn…"

"Phil's gay?" Caesar asked incredulously. "I've known him all my life."

Quinn deadpanned.

"Pull it out," she demanded.

"Okay," he conceded, unzipping his fly and beginning what seemed to be a Herculean task of freeing himself from his pants.

"Stop!" Quinn said, as she saw the meat of the thing begin to emerge. Heads turned, then lowered. Caesar looked confused, at the point of either pulling it out further or pushing it back. As he noticed that the more interested faces did indeed seem to be men, he hesitated, then pushed it back in. Quinn was shaking her head in what seemed to be disgust.

"You told me to pull it out," he said simply.

"I wanted to see if you'd do it," she said sounding, strangely, a bit winded.

Caesar shrugged.

"You would have, wouldn't you?" she asked, not really incredulous, more like interested.

Caesar shrugged again.

"I'm not ashamed of it," he said offhandedly.

How could you be? Quinn asked without speaking.

"Pull your titties out," he commanded, more as a prank than as anything else. In one motion, the halter was snatched forward then down and there seemed to be an explosion of heaving brown flesh and nipples.

"Goddamn!" some nigga screamed as the things that perhaps only he and Caesar caught a full glimpse of disappeared quickly from sight. Other cats just caught them being stuffed quickly back into the halter-top. Caesar seemed struck blind.

"I've never seen anything like those before," he said, shaking his head in smirking disbelief after his eyesight had been fully restored.

"Shut up, boy," Quinn said playfully. "You saw them twice before."

"Yeah, but the lighting was bad," Caesar lamented. "I didn't get a full appreciation of them. They're wonderful."

Quinn smiled confidently.

"Want to get outta here and fuck?" she asked, as she grabbed herself by the bottom of her breasts and pushed them completely back into place.

"Yeah, but…"

Quinn quickly grabbed Caesar by the wrist and led him out of the joint, saying record-breaking quick good-byes to Carmen and Steeze, who were dirty dancing with different partners right next to each other. She never heard the but.

"His daughter?"

Quinn nodded. Her expression was as flat as Carmen had ever seen it.

"I never heard no man make no excuse like that," Carmen continued, shaking her head. Quinn deadpanned. "You think he was just trying to get you back?" Carmen asked.

"What do you think?" Quinn asked hotly.

"Well…" Carmen moaned.

Quinn had been almost salivating. She had never said anything as forward to a man as she had said to Caesar that night. And it was about to come to pass. She wouldn't need foreplay. She felt oceans move between her legs and figured that if he didn't drive any faster, she might in fact need to towel herself off before they began. Then they got there.

She hadn't even bothered to turn on the lights. She just began undressing, using her right hand to pull off her own clothes and her left hand to pull off his. He was standing at attention. She couldn't figure out how she wanted to do it, so she simply jumped into his arms while he was standing, reached down and began to maneuver that thing towards the place where she hoped it would stay for a long, long time.

"Hold up for a second," he said, as she held him by the base, positioning him for the plunge.

She frowned bitterly.

"Hold up for what?" she asked.

"We can't do this," he said.

"Can't do what?" she asked. He must have been talking about the position, she quickly theorized. As far as she was concerned, the act was a foregone conclusion.

"Can't have sex," he said simply.

Quinn's face chanced from incredulous to a strange, distant, almost foreign sadness, before disintegrating into disgust. Her hand released him and, as she climbed down from having her legs wrapped around his waist, her right thigh pushed his member downward until it sprung back upward like a pinball flipper. She would have laughed at the sight had she not been so devastated. Then, she brightened quickly.

"Oh," she said cheerily. "I know what's wrong. You forgot yours? I almost forgot to offer, I got so caught up in the moment." She raced into the bedroom and came back with an assortment.

"It's not condoms," Caesar said evenly before reaching out to inspect some of the brands that she had brought with her from the room. "But thank you."

Quinn angrily slapped the rubbers out of his hands.

"Put those down," she said as the batch hit the floor. "If you ain't using 'em on me, buy your own."

Caesar chuckled a little.

"Why can't we do it?" Quinn asked angrily, sounding quickly, frighteningly, and almost sexily like a man. Caesar inhaled deep.

"I want you to meet my daughter," he said evenly. The two sides of Quinn's face delivered two different messages. On one side she was honored and surprised by this traditional man with purposeful family values. On the other she felt clowned by this fool who wouldn't have sex with her. She took a step back, away from Caesar, sure that his eyesight must have been suffering if he could choose, after seeing her naked, not to have sex with her. He appraised her, head to toe, grabbing himself in a vice grip and looking around on the floor for his underwear. He was serious, thought Quinn, as she watched him begin to dress. She couldn't believe it.

"I can't believe it," Carmen said shaking her head.

"I think it's all bullshit," Quinn said, with anger at the corners of her tone.

Carmen frowned.

"You think he's just trying to get you back for going off to do the record that night?" she asked.

Quinn nodded slowly.

"And that's some petty shit," she said shaking her head. "I told him how much money was involved. He knows how much I could use it. It wasn't like I was choosing between him or the money forever. I could get with him anytime. But right then was the only chance I had to get the money."

"And do a song with Bay-B," Carmen said lustily.

"Yeah..." Quinn moaned in remembrance.

"Did you ask him about his dick?" Carmen asked eagerly. Quinn frowned bitterly.

"No," she concluded. "He did ask me what I was doing after we finished recording though."

"What'd you say?" Carmen asked, her eyes bright enough to light the night.

"I said I was just going home. I thought Caesar was there waiting for me."

"Did you tell Caesar that?" Quinn frowned.

"No," she said, the wheels of her mind turning furiously through her eyes. "That's another thing. I might have been able to get with Bay-B and I turned down the chance to go running to his ass!"

Carmen breathed a silent moan through circled lips.

"Would you do it again?" she asked.

"In a heartbeat," Quinn said without pause.

Caesar was shirtless, sitting at the edge of his bed in his boxer shorts, thinking. It was almost four o'clock in the morning. He didn't know what had woke him, but whatever it was had set his mind in motion. Now it wouldn't stop.

He had always been hesitant to bring women around Champagne. He didn't want his little girl to see him with the type of women he usually associated with. Not that they were actual paid whores, just that they usually serviced an urge. Little more. The girls who sneak in at the most impossible hour past his sleeping mother and child would have the craziest variations of hair colors and nail contraptions. They'd have miniskirts without panties, baby T-shirts without bras and, sometimes, long skirt and Timberland boot combinations. They knew what they were there for.

Of course, Champagne knew Toni, the girl who didn't suck dick. Champagne even seemed to like Toni. It was either because she genuinely did like Toni or because it seemed to mean so much to her father that she do, Caesar never knew. Even then, Caesar had been hesitant to introduce Champagne to Toni. He wanted to make sure that Toni would be around for a while first. Champagne, Caesar already knew, wasn't going anywhere.

She had come from a one-night stand, his daughter a girl with the name of a beverage. This wild girl he'd had a fling with had turned up pregnant. Caesar didn't know about her until the girl was almost three years old. When he found out, went to see the child with eyes that seemed to be a mirror reflection of his, he took one look around at the surroundings and decided that the only way that this child could be properly raised was by him. There wasn't no court battles or anything. Now, he felt he might be introducing his daughter to the stepmother he had always hoped he'd find for her. Moreover, Quinn was seemingly the woman he'd always been looking for himself. But he didn't want to get ahead of himself. He didn't want to get all into her only to find out that she and Champagne couldn't get along. He wanted to get them together in one place, make sure they had no major personality conflicts then decide if this was a thing he could do. Served Quinn right, he thought, shaking his head as he rose from the edge of his bed. The way she had made him wait as she ran off to make a record with that nigga Bay-B.

"I hate that fuckin' faggot," Shortie breathed hot. She wasn't looking at Quinn, who was looking exclusively at her. Quinn said nothing. "I mean, to actually catch him with a man," Shortie continued.

Quinn raised an eyebrow. Uh-oh, she thought, wanting to smile or laugh but preventing herself from doing either.

"What were they doing?" Quinn asked, trying her best to straighten her voice into something that sounded like it didn't contain any of the mockery she was feeling right at that moment. Shortie looked her in the eye for the first time since she had shown up at the door and breathed a long, slow sigh.

"Dred was on his knees," she began, her eyes now in the memory and talking as if she was narrating something she was actually seeing as she spoke. "And there was this little dude behind him," she continued. "This little dude who was on his knees too. And the little dude kept bending his body between Dred's legs and twisting to suck his dick, then coming back out from under and sticking his tongue in his ass." Quinn frowned at the idea of the sight.

"And he kept doing it over and over again," Shortie continued. "Till finally… I dunno, I guess he got himself hard or something, but he grabs his own dick, put it behind Dred and then…"

"He fucked him?" Phil Flarn asked incredulously. Then he started laughing uncontrollably. So uncontrollably in fact that he dropped the phone, doubled over and kept laughing until Quinn could hear nothing but the sounds of the dying man.

Joyce picked up the phone.

"Forgive Phil," Joyce said to Quinn as Phil Flarn's laughter continued to echo in the background.

"Doesn't matter," Quinn said into the phone. "What were you two doing?"

"Oh, we were just thinking about going to dinner or something. There's a comedy night down on 125th street and there's also this new movie I wanted to check out…"

"No! No!" Phil Flarn warned, coming out of his laughter. "Let me speak to Quinn again. I gotta get the rest of the story."

Joyce eyed him with mild disgust.

"Quinn, do you wanna talk to this moron?" she asked.

Quinn didn't actually want to talk to anybody. She had to talk. But her options were so limited, what without Shortie being the friend she once was and the fact that her talk would directly involve Shortie. It wasn't something she could imagine going to her parents with. Life had never known that she had had a lesbian relationship even though he had met Shortie on a couple of occasions and, for some reason, possibly out of fear of her own temptations, she had never gotten Carmen's number. So she called Joyce. That asshole: Phil Flarn just happened to be there. He had commandeered the phone when Joyce seemed to be getting too into the conversation.

"Put him on," Quinn said tiredly.

Phil Flarn grabbed the phone, smiling eagerly.

"So what happened next?" he asked excitedly.

"Well, she said the guy who was fucking her man was somebody we both know," Quinn said.

"Who?" Phil Flarn asked quickly.

"The drummer," Quinn said evenly.

"Trent?" Phil Flarn asked.

Quinn nodded. Then she realized that a nod couldn't be heard over the phone and said, "Yep." Then Phil Flarn's laughter started up again.

"I'm sorry," Joyce said tiredly, coming to the phone as the sounds of Phil's death rang hollow. He seemed to be dying in all parts of the apartment.

"So what movie are y'all going to check out?" Quinn asked, now eager to change the subject. She had done her part, relieved herself of her burden and was now eager to act like dishing this dirt had only been part of the reason for her call.

"I dunno," Joyce said frowning. "There's not too many good ones out right now. Phil'll watch anything. That's why I'm really leaning towards dinner or the comedy thing…"

"Nooooo!" Phil said, alive again. "Gimme the phone."

This time, Joyce handed it over without asking for

Quinn's permission.

"So Trent was the Top?" Phil Flarn asked with renewed interest.

"How do you know such terms?" Quinn asked skeptically.

"That's not like a big gay secret or anything," Phil Flarn said, bunching his face up. "The Top is the dude doing the fucking, the Bottom is the dude getting it done to him. If you watch enough talk shows you'll find that out."

"Didn't know you were a talk show kind of guy, Phil," Quinn said, now trying to rattle him.

"I'm not," Phil Flarn said. "I'm a Bottom. Joyce is the Top. Now will you tell me more about the man-love, please?"

"Why are you so interested?" Quinn asked.

"Because I am," Phil Flarn said flatly. "Tell me everything she told you."

"And he was pounding away," Shortie had said. "Pounding him like a man fucks a woman he don't like."

Quinn recoiled at the image Shortie's words were leaving in her mind.

"Where were you all this time?" she asked. "I mean, how were you able to watch?"

"I had just come home," Shortie said. "They were in the bedroom with their backs to me. I was able to watch the whole thing without either of them noticing."

"Why'd you watch the whole thing?" Quinn asked, it seeming pretty obvious that the sight had disturbed her former friend.

Shortie began shaking her head.

"I just couldn't believe it," she said, her eyes blank with disbelief. "I mean, I always knew he had gay tendencies, but I thought that all he really needed was somebody to act like a man for him. To be tough, you know? But if what he needs is what that kid was giving him…" she shook her head again. "I don't even think that I could give it to him with a dildo."

Quinn shook her head too. She turned away so that Shortie could not see the ridiculously big grin growing across her face. Then she turned back.

"Girl, I'm sorry," she said with all the sincerity she could fake. Shortie rushed over to her. Quinn wrapped her arms around the shorter woman and held her close.

Quinn had known who it was from the beginning when she heard the obscenely loud banging at the door. Only Shortie was rude enough to bang like that. Quinn didn't rush to the door but walked quickly, pausing for a minute to throw on some shorts. She was only wearing panties when the knocking started and knowing it was Shortie, there was no way that she wanted to go the door in her panties. She opened up. Shortie was in tears. As much as she would have wanted to enjoy the sight, it actually threw her off a bit to see her former friend like that. Still, they didn't touch. Quinn simply led her inside and offered her a seat.

"So what happened next?" Phil Flarn asked Quinn. "I mean, like, did they see her or something?"

"Yeah," Quinn said. "The drummer saw her. She said she stepped unevenly on a floorboard or something and, when it squeaked, he turned around."

"What happened then?" Phil Flarn asked.

"When he turned, his dick came out of Dred," Shortie said to Quinn. "And it was huge."

Quinn shook her head, imagining the little-ass drummer with a big-ass dick.

"It was so big," Shortie continued, "that it looked like a grown man's forearm swaying there from his waist."

Quinn shook her head again, imagining the monstrosity that Shortie was describing. Shortie continued.

"Then the guy's like, 'Hey, you must be Shortie. I've heard a lot about you. Wanna join in'?"

"What'd she do?" Phil Flarn asked Quinn, his eyes popping out of his head through his voice on the phone.

"I couldn't resist," Shortie said to Quinn. "I didn't feel any loyalty to Dred anymore. Besides, that thing was so big, I just had to experience it."

"She fucked Trent?" Phil Flarn asked incredulously.

"Not only that," Quinn began. "But while the drummer was hitting her from behind, he was also sucking Dred's dick."

"Ugh," Phil Flarn moaned, disgusted. "What kind of friends do you have?"

"My friends?" Quinn asked. "Isn't the drummer your man?"

"Yeah," Phil Flarn said defensively. "And I gotta admit, I'm kinda proud of him. He's gettin' pussy now and all. But your girl and her man..." Phil Flarn paused to shake his head as if Quinn could see him over the phone, "they're nasty."

Quinn breathed an exasperated exhale.

"Put Joyce back on the phone," she said.

Phil Flarn handed the phone over without a word.

"So Shortie fucked the drummer and her man, huh?" Joyce asked, her words screeching over the idea like a bad DJ.

"Basically," Quinn said, thankful for her friend's frankness.

"How do you feel about it?" Joyce asked.

Quinn really didn't know how she felt. Or rather, she knew, but wasn't ready to admit it to herself yet. She had worked as hard as she could not to hate Shortie. Not to wish hateful shit upon Shortie.

"God bless her," she always said aloud whenever the thought of Shortie, Dred or the baby they were both about to have came into her mind. But in reality, she wished that God would curse them. Maybe not with anything truly evil like a problem birth or AIDS or some shit like that, but maybe with herpes or a bad skin rash or lost jobs all around or arrests and convictions on either part for crimes that weren't committed. She wished them bad luck. A lifetime of it. That would only be justice, she figured. Considering the way that Shortie had made her feel.

So when Shortie had come to the door and Quinn could see the problems in her old friend's eyes, she felt instantly vindicated. Quinn didn't even have to hear the story to know that her wishes of limited evil had been granted. And after she did indeed hear the story, she understood why she prayed sometimes. God was good, Quinn thought. What went around had come back around. And with no more velocity or animosity than she, Quinn, would have wanted.

After Shortie had finished telling Quinn the story, there was a moment that the two women stood staring at each other across the distance of Quinn's living room. Both knew what the other was thinking. They were remembering the times when that same living room had been like a safe haven from the world for the two of them. They were remembering a time when, even though Shortie never lived with Quinn, her presence was as sure as the furnishings. They were remembering a time when they loved each other openly and purely. Now that time was gone.

"Quinn..." Shortie began, her voice softer than Quinn remembered possible. "What happened to us?"

Her eyes were wide and trembling. Tears threatened to fill them from the bottom up. Quinn looked at her, not quite incredulous, but kind of dubious. Shortie took off running. It was all Quinn could do not to be knocked over by her when she arrived. She came jumping, leaping up into Quinn's arms much like Quinn had leaped into Caesar's that night. Quinn surprised herself with her own strength in catching Shortie, then slowly, gently, lowered her back to the flow. In an instant, Shortie's mouth was pressed to hers and her tongue was digging, reaching inside of Quinn's lips. They were met with teeth. Rows and rows of teeth. After a short while, Shortie got the message.

"It's over between us, huh?" she asked, finding her old lover unwilling to open her mouth for a tongue kiss.

"That is," Quinn said, referring to the time when their love was physical.

"What do we have then?" Shortie asked.

Quinn shrugged.

"I don't know," she said simply and noticed that the tone of her own words was sincere. She didn't know. She knew what they had, but didn't know what was there now. She didn't know how she felt about Shortie or herself in relation to Shortie. And strangely, she sensed without even acknowledging to herself, she didn't care.

It was funny. She had known from the beginning that Shortie would be back. Shortie had done her wrong. It wasn't that she had begrudged Shortie for finding a man, but the way Shortie had gone about breaking the news to her had been heartbreaking. It was like Shortie had done it intentionally, to see if she could break her heart. She could and did. Quinn had wondered what kind of perverse pleasure Shortie had derived from this. She wondered if Shortie had considered her some great tease for all the years they'd known each other and had promised herself from the beginning that if she ever did sleep with Quinn, she'd pay her back for making her wait. And Quinn thought about it. Had she teased Shortie? Had she lingered or pranced around in her bras or, worse yet, without a bra when she knew that the thing that Shortie craved the most aside from eating her out was sucking her titties? And had she known? Had she really known? She had caught Shortie casting sideways glances at her enough to know that the possibility was there, but was the knowledge there? Did she know? She shook her head.

True, the idea had always turned her on a little. The thought that Shortie might be checking her out had always kept her nipples erect when she was topless. She would talk, her breasts bouncing heavy, nipples as diamonds, about everything but the fact that her heavy breasts were bouncing and her nipples were as hard as diamonds. She could see something in Shortie's eyes. The way they gleamed, the way she looked away purposely but with difficulty as if the thing she wanted most was to grab, kiss and caress them. Sometimes Quinn had wished she would. She had wished that Shortie would grab her by the shoulders and force her mouth to those things, her teeth between a bite and a graze, her tongue fast at work, licking as if varying tastes were coming with each stroke.

She'd say, "Stop Shortie. What are you doing?" after she'd had enough time to enjoy it. It would only take a moment. The real victory would have been in making Shortie lose it. She could get any nigga to suck her titties. But Shortie never did lose it. She remained composed even as those massive breasts swung heavy in her face, sometimes wincing to avoid an aggressive nipple that it seemed might poke her in the eye.

It seemed that Shortie was teasing Quinn when they did finally start fucking, obsessed with Quinn's vagina. It was like she was ignoring those breasts. They experienced almost a full month of sex before Shortie had put her mouth on them. But once she finally did, she never stopped. And then, to leave her so abruptly…

Quinn took a deep breath, then spoke.

"We can be friends," she said simply. "Just like before." Shortie looked sincerely relieved. They hugged.

"I feel okay," Quinn said to Joyce, hearing the doubt in

her own voice and sure that Joyce could hear it too.

"Why not good?" Joyce asked.

Quinn was silent. Finally, she exhaled.

"I feel stupid 'cause I feel for Shortie," she said finally. Joyce was shaking her head where she sat. "Like, I feel like I should hate her or something, but I can't," Quinn continued.

"That's good," Joyce said firmly. "You should try not to hate anybody." Then she started laughing. "I know I'm talking shit," Joyce continued laughing. "But if it was me, I'd probably hate her ass. It's good of you not to, though."

Quinn felt better. She had wanted to feel good, but at least she felt better. Joyce had let her know that it was alright to hate Shortie, now she could feel like she was taking the high road by not doing so.

"Thank you," she said to Joyce. "Thank Phil for me too. He tried, I guess…" With that she hung up. She thought about Shortie. She wanted to call her, to talk to her because she knew Shortie needed a friend. She was pregnant by a man she wasn't gonna keep and with a baby she wasn't sure about keeping. She had left Quinn's apartment with about as much doubt as she had arrived with, with one exception: she knew she had a friend again. But Quinn knew there was a delicate balance. She wanted to be there for Shortie, she wanted to be a friend, but she didn't want to get close enough to her to get hurt again. Moreover, she didn't wanna get close enough again to make Shortie think she could hurt her again and it would be all good. She sat alone, wondering what to do and who to call. The answer was nothing and nobody. Then when she found herself all alone, it seemed finally as if she had begun to understand something; she was all she had. And it wasn't as if the thought had never occurred to her, it was just that whenever that particular thought had made itself a possibility in her own mind, she pushed it away, terrified. But now she accepted it. And in accepting it, felt strength and, strangely, comfort. If she was all alone, she couldn't think of anybody she'd rather be with. The phone rang. It was Alanda. She hadn't seen or heard from that bitch since the night she had recorded with Bay-B.

"So, what's the deal?" Quinn asked, with a tone she hoped would let the bitch know that her call wasn't particularly welcome.

"You," Alanda said simply.

"Meaning?" Quinn asked.

"Meaning you're hot to death," Alanda said. "Bay-B let a lot of muh'fuckas hear that song you did with him and they're all open. You know how many calls I got asking for your number and your manager? I got your number. Do you got a manager?"

No. Quinn would not do R&B. She had thought she had made herself clear. As good as Alanda's offer had sounded and as broke as she was, she still wasn't gonna compromise her principles. She was a jazz singer. Would Etta James be caught dead warbling over a Timbaland-produced track? Not that she was Etta James. The point was, she wasn't Monifah either. It had been hours since she had hung up the phone with Joyce, hours more since Shortie had left. She had wanted to have sex with Shortie. She had left that part out when she had been talking to Joyce and even when she had been alone in her thoughts. Something about Shortie's vulnerability had been sexy to her. Something about seeing the tough girl stripped of her toughness made her wanna for once, be the man in a sexual exchange with the girl. But she knew that only hell could come of it. Either Shortie, careening on the rebound, would take the gesture as ignition to their now lifeless physical relationship, or Quinn herself wouldn't derive the power she expected to experience, and would feel cheated: used. Sex was rarely the answer to anything when love wasn't the question and there were only two people in the world that she could think of that she might have loved right then.

"You turned it down?" Carmen asked incredulously the next morning. Quinn nodded. Carmen shook her head.

"I'm over here writing for *Tiger Beat* magazine with dreams of one day writing for *Vanity Fair* and you're turning down an opportunity that could one day lead to you becoming the next Billy D. Williams."

"Billie Holiday," Quinn corrected.

Carmen looked confused.

"Billy D. Williams was Lando in *Star Wars*," Quinn continued.

Carmen nodded, remembering.

"Anyway," Carmen began again, "isn't the point to get your foot in the door?"

"Not that door," Quinn said shaking her head.

Carmen shrugged.

"Guess you know what you're doing," she said finally. "Tell me more about Shortie."

Telling Carmen about her experience the night before with Shortie had been totally different from telling Joyce. For one, Carmen felt no ill-regard about wishing on death and disease.

"I wish that bitch would die coughing," she said at one point after hearing how Shortie had had the nerve to make advances towards Quinn after just telling her that she had joined in one of the weirdest ménages à trois anybody had ever heard of.

"How dare she come to you with her problems?"

Quinn shook her head. She had always loved Carmen's passion. That may have been the main thing she had always been attracted to in the girl. Her ability to love and feel so recklessly. Carmen would fall hard many times throughout her life, Quinn could foresee, but she would also rise and rise again.

"Come here. Let me touch your titties," Carmen said in a voice that was so low it took Quinn by surprise.

"You know Bill is upstairs watching," Quinn warned, her own voice low.

"I just wanna touch 'em," Carmen said, her voice becoming even lower.

Quinn's nipples shot out to hard erections. She walked as if in a trance towards Carmen. Carmen held her hands out in front of her in anticipation. Then, when Quinn was close enough, she made contact. Nobody was surprised when a loud crash was heard from upstairs. Instead, the lovers just played on through. Carmen's hands moved quickly along Quinn's waist and Quinn reached out with an anger she didn't know the source of to grip Carmen hard by the buttocks. She dug her nails in tight and as she slid her knee between Carmen's thigh, Carmen backed away, holding Quinn at a distance by the shoulders. She quickly slid her stretch pants down around her ankles, spun around and hopped up on the counter behind her, belly-first. Quinn placed her hands flat, one each along Carmen's tremendous cheeks, poked out her tongue, and surged forward.

"What the fuck?" a voice all too familiar to Carmen erupted in the store. Carmen's cheeks quickly tightened around Quinn's nose.

"Steeze?" she pleaded as she turned around and into a sitting position on the counter.

"What the fuck are y'all doin'?" Steeze asked, his voice somewhere between anger and fear. Quinn began wiping down her face with her hand.

"Yeah," Bill asked, emerging along the stairs, rubbing left hand across the back of his pants. "What was that? That couldn't have been no movie. At least, not the kind you gotta rehearse for."

"We were just fooling around," Quinn offered weakly, once she felt herself clean.

"Obviously," Steeze and Bill offered simultaneously.

"Look Steeze," Carmen began, her eyes wide with honesty, "I love Quinn. I want to have sex with her too. I wanna have sex with her because I love her. She's beautiful, she's smart, she's funny, and she's talented. As far as I'm concerned, those are all good reasons to both love somebody and wanna have sex with them. Much better than the bullshit reasons you be using to get with all them chicken-headed bitches you be fuckin'."

Steeze opened his mouth to speak, but closed it again. He shook his head instead.

"You gotta choose," he said finally. "You gotta choose between me and her."

"Why I gotta choose when you're still gonna be fucking mad bitches?" Carmen demanded.

"I'm gonna quit," Steeze said evenly. "That's what I was coming by here to tell you today. I'm gonna quit fuckin' around. I love you Carmen and I can't stand the thought of anybody else having you."

"That's why you're gonna quit?" Carmen asked dubiously.

Steeze shook his head.

"No," he said simply. "I love you and I don't wanna be with anybody else."

"Steeze," Carmen cheered, hopping up off the counter her pants and panties still around her ankles, the sight of her bush causing Bill to double over from the pain of a sudden new erection. Carmen hopped over to Steeze, her bottom half still exposed. She jumped up into his arms, wrapping her hands around the back of his neck. He grabbed her by the top of the ass, then slid his hands downward, ending up cupping the bottom of her behind as he pulled her up and closer to him.

Their tongues looked like they were fighting each other, surfacing outside of each mouth and then returning inside to fight some more. Bill scurried off to his office where he could enjoy the scene from a safe vantage point. Steeze placed Carmen on a lower table, one about waist high, pulling her pants and panties all the way off. He backed away. Next went his pants and Quinn nearly gasped at the uprising of his penis. It rose high and angry and headed, it seemed, right for the lighting. She watched it as it moved forward now; it swayed with each step seeming to aim itself at what it knew to be its own destination. Then it dug in. He almost seemed to be swimming the way his back arched as he moved, the side of his shaft becoming evident with the distance he left between himself and Carmen's vagina with each stroke. Quinn couldn't take it any more. She pulled down her own pants and found herself overflowing with oceans of wet. Her breasts were raging and in a move she reserved for only the most special of sexual occasions, she pulled one out, and commenced to sucking and biting its nipple.

"WHAT THE FUCK?" came the last voice that anybody wanted to hear. It was that asshole: Phil Flarn, hand-in-hand with Joyce and Joyce's daughter. Steeze and Carmen ignored them. They continued fucking, the residue from their friction beginning to soak the shirts at the side of the counter on which their action was taking place. Quinn quickly pulled up her pants and lowered her shirt. She stood up to greet her friend and that asshole: Phil Flarn. Joyce had the look of a woman suddenly stuck in a scene from a foreign language film. Phil Flarn was shaking his head.

"We just came by to check on you..." Joyce said as if she'd had the words paused in her mind since the idea of visiting Quinn had occurred to her and someone had just now hit the pause button.

"Looks like you're doing all right," Phil Flarn said.

"Mommy, what are they doing?" Joyce's little girl Hey-Hey asked.

"Making a mess on a stack of new shirts," Phil Flarn intervened to say.

"Don't look at that," Joyce said, shielding Hey-Hey's eyes.

"Why not?" Phil Flarn asked. "They're doing it right."

Joyce shot Phil a murderous look.

"C'mon," Phil said to Hey-Hey, snatching the little girl up in his arms and carrying her out the store.

Joyce and Quinn stood silent for a moment, eyeing each other. Quinn shook her head, looking for words.

"If I had to explain every situation I'd ever been in, in my life, I'd be at a loss too," Joyce said and with that, Quinn's head stopped shaking. She nodded a thank you. "You okay?" Joyce asked.

Quinn nodded again.

"See you later in that case," Joyce said, then left.

"How's this weekend sound?" Caesar asked.

Quinn had been so happy to hear his voice. Watching Steeze and Carmen earlier that day had made her so horny that she had almost called Life. She knew it would have been a mistake, but it would have been about as bad as a dieter having one more piece of chocolate: she'd quit tomorrow for good.

"Sounds really good," Quinn said, hoping that Caesar didn't hear the eagerness in her tone. Memories of Steeze yanking out his member and watching him erupt violently leaving trails of white saliva along Carmen's naked stomach, were on Quinn's mind as her hand began making its way down her pelvis.

"Okay then. Saturday I'll come and pick you up."

"Okay," Quinn said. She hung up. Come now, she was thinking. There was a knock at the door.

Think of the devil…

She opened the door.

"Hi Quinn," Life said in the tone that had made her fall in love with his voice originally.

"Life," Quinn said, trying her best to sound indifferently surprised. "What brings you by?" Her body was raging. She half-hoped that he would just rip her clothes off and put it in. She other half-hoped he'd jump out of her window and die. She hardened. "Didn't I tell you to never just drop by?" she asked, her brow furrowed, her voice in a tone intended to let him know that she didn't take kindly to his intrusion.

He nodded.

"I just wanted to see you," he said simply.

"And I just want a million dollars," Quinn said quickly. "See, we can't always have what we want."

Life wrinkled his lips.

"I'm sorry for all the things I did wrong, Quinn," he said. For a moment, Quinn was taken aback. Life had never apologized for anything. Somebody else had always been responsible for his mistakes. "I just want another chance," he continued.

Quinn squinted to look at him through new eyes. It was as if she was seeing him for the first time.

"Why this? Why now?" she asked honestly. The proposition of a caring Life was something that had to be explored further.

He shrugged.

"I just looked at my life the way it is," he began, "and I realized that things were going good when I had you, but then when you were gone everything started going wrong."

Quinn took a deep breath. She didn't know how to feel.

"What about me?" she asked suddenly.

Life's face dug into itself.

"What about me?" Quinn asked again.

"What do you mean?" Life asked.

"What about me?" she repeated. "What about my life? What about the way it was when you were here versus the way it is now?"

Life was confused. Quinn continued.

"I mean, you come in here because of the way you feel about your life, but you never stopped to wonder about me. If I'm any better with you or without you."

Life's eyes went wide.

"Well…" he began.

"I'm not," Quinn said, cutting him off. "Better with you, that is. I'm better without you."

Life looked as if he'd been shot. And it was his mother holding the gun.

"I'm not blaming you because I was with you," Quinn continued. "But you sure as hell didn't make my life any better. Not that I expected you to. My time with you was just… wasted."

Life's mouth parted slowly, the space left in his lips leaving his face looking bewildered. He had not expected this. He had always believed that though Quinn had initiated their break-up, he could reconcile with her anytime he wanted to. Time, after all, was on his side. She was getting older. She was thirty. Her biological clock was ticking. She needed him. But here she was telling him in no uncertain terms that she didn't want him back. That she didn't need him. That her clock could keep ticking forever for all she cared because if it was up to him to stop it, then it just wouldn't stop. Strangely enough, she had never been as attractive to him as right then. Sure, in the beginning he had thought he had her all figured out, a skinny, big-tittied girl with a lot of pent-up frustration that in all reality only needed some good, hard dick. And time had revealed some nuances to her, but his assessment had remained essentially the same. And he knew that he could return because his dick would always be good. But now she was turning it down; his dick and himself. He wondered if she really knew what she was doing. He decided to try his luck.

"You know that if I leave tonight, I'm never coming back?" he asked, his tone more in a threat than in a question.

Quinn got up, she walked over to the door, she opened it and she used her free hand to gesture that she'd like him to follow the path that it carved through the air. Life looked at her incredulously. He stood up. He began walking towards Quinn and the door. At the door he paused.

"I'm really gonna go," he said.

"Bye," Quinn said.

He walked out shaking his head.

Quinn walked over to her bed, lay down flat, crossed her arms along her chest and trapped her elbows with her knees.

God, Caesar had better be good for what she had just turned down…

You're coming to your apocalypse," Carmen said the next day. Quinn's eyes went haywire, too tired to be incredulous.

"First Shortie, then the offer from Alanda, then Life..." Carmen began, shaking her head "Some real shit's about to happen to you next. Quinn shook her head and went back to work. When Cedric showed up at her apartment that night, Carmen was the first person she thought about.

"Where did we go wrong, Quinn?" he asked once Quinn had allowed him all the way into the apartment. Quinn's mouth was wide open as if she were either about to eat something or she had just been asked a question she couldn't believe was expectant of an answer.

"We loved each other once, didn't we?" he continued. Quinn's features all rushed to join in the middle of her face.

"Cedric, what are you talking about?" she asked as if searching for a meaning in his words that hadn't made itself evident as he had spoken them.

"Let's get married again," he said flatly, as Quinn's eyes seemed to follow something that had just flown out the window.

"Why?" was all that she could bring herself to say.

"I just looked at my life the way it is," he began, "and I realized that things were going good when I had you, but then when you were gone, everything started going wrong."

She looked at him deadpan and blinked, twice.

"You've gotta be kidding," she said after a moment had passed. She started to ask him if he knew Life and if the two of them had rehearsed their lines before they had each come to her, but she shook the idea off. These two men were just at the same stage in their existences, she decided. And they had both concluded that the point in their lives at which everything had taken a turn for the worse was the point at which she had ceased being a part. She should have been flattered.

"Get the fuck out," she said quite deliberately.

Cedric looked stunned at first.

"You know that if I leave tonight, I'm never coming back?" he asked, his tone more in a threat than in a question.

Quinn got up, she walked over to the door, she opened it and she used her free hand to gesture that she'd like him to follow the path that it carved through the air. Cedric stood up. He began walking towards Quinn and the door. At the door he paused.

"I'm really gonna go," he said.

"I know, I know," Quinn said tiredly. She slammed the door behind him. This time though, she didn't go over to her bed and curl up in a ball. She just sat down on the sofa and waited for more signs of the apocalypse.

Saturday came before Quinn had a chance to prepare herself for it and before she knew it, she was in Caesar's car headed up the FDR and on her way to New London, New York. It felt good to be getting out of the city. She needed a break sometimes from the race that she ran in her own life, and today was one of those days. She couldn't imagine the people for whom there were no breaks, for whom the city was reality 24-7. She'd see them and it would be reflected in their eyes, the fact that there was no end or relief in sight. You just had to find a place, she thought to herself as even the filth of the East River to her right seemed cleansed by the newness of the day. Even if that place was internal. Lord knew she had escaped into the recesses of her own mind enough. Her mind was like a vault to which only she had the key and which upon being unlocked provided her with many places to hide. Today she didn't need any of them though. Today she was going to meet Caesar's daughter, and if luck were on her side, later on, she'd be meeting the rest of Caesar.

"You ever been Upstate?" he asked, startling her with his voice. It was as if she had forgotten he could speak. Him, there at the steering wheel, had become nothing more than a part of her scenery.

"Uh… I been to Bear Mountain," she said after thinking heavy on the subject.

"We're not that far up," he said. His tone was nervous. She understood why. It was important to him that she and his daughter get along well. She couldn't have ever told him that it really didn't matter to her. Sure, it would be ideal if they could be one big happy family for as long as they were together, but who knew how long that was gonna be? In the interim, she was satisfied to be just the woman that daddy was sleeping with. Hell, after Life, Cedric and Alanda's offers, the last thing in the world Quinn was ready to think about was a relationship.

The car whizzed across the George Washington Bridge, Caesar tentatively at the wheel. Quinn had the sudden impulse to just blow him right then. To just pull the thing out of his pants and get it over with. That would have settled him down a little, she figured. She had abandoned her desire to paint an image for him. Whatever type of woman he was gonna think she was, he'd just have to think it. Why did she have to go through this bullshit anyway? Why was she the one who had to be ashamed of anything in the past that she had done? He had probably eaten out a girl's ass or been the recipient of a golden shower or two. Hell, he might have even done a guy at one point in his life. But whereas his missteps and thoughts could be ignored or even bragged about, every penis she sucked had been attached a number and each increase in that number called for a decrease in the amount of respect she was supposed to be afforded.

Quinn sighed and reclined further in her seat as trees replaced the bridge and city backdrop. The truth seemed to be such a scary proposition. Before she knew it, she was in a town that seemed to be conceptualized by some white artist who wished to depict the type of place all of his perversions might come up with. It was vast and hollowed, encompassing homes of all types with no centrality of theme or purpose. There were pizza places and antique stores, bars constructed for alcoholic white suburbanites and thrift shops without the promise of thrift. There were delis, seemingly by the thousands, and banks that seemed to have been built for money intake only, never as institutions of loan. The roads were wide with cars parked even on the main thoroughfares. The people on the streets, black, white and of colors and origins unknown, apparently understood their respective roles, and seemed hesitant to venture outside of them. It was a small town, yes, but New York could be felt lingering like a threat somewhere near. Quinn didn't like it.

They pulled up in front of a house, white, quaint, and quite squat actually, and parked. This must have been the place. Quinn would have never allowed herself to understand how nervous she was. She wouldn't have even known that the gnawing inside of her to just go ahead and do something, even if it was something as drastic as sucking Caesar off as he drove, was just a product of that nervousness. But now she was outside of the car approaching the house, hand in hand with Caesar and scared to death. And it seemed so irrational. What did a grown woman have to be afraid of from a little girl? What was the worst that the girl could do to her? Not like her? She could just as easily not like the girl. But the girl did have one advantage over her. Liked or not, at the end of the day, the girl would have Caesar whereas she was only now coming to realize how much she wished she could say the same.

Quinn followed Caesar inside and up the stairs. She tried to see as much of the house that she was passing as she could but it pretty much went by in a blur. She noticed family pictures as she passed the living room to her left. A light-skinned fifty-ish woman with Caesar's smile just had to be his mother. The stairs were narrow and hard to follow. Then Quinn saw Caesar's eyes again. And his smile. They were both being worn on the face of his daughter. The girl's eyes brightened as they took Quinn in.

"This your girlfriend, daddy?" Champagne asked Caesar as if the woman would be hers not his.

"Hopefully," Caesar said.

"She's ugly," Champagne countered, at which point Quinn's face hit the floor.

That little bitch.

"Just kidding," Champagne said quickly. "She'll do."

It was early spring now and so the trio that found themselves all in short sleeves really felt as if the world was their oyster. Thoughts of a movie were shot down quickly by both Quinn and Champagne, who couldn't imagine wasting a beautiful day by spending it inside a dark, cramped movie theatre. So they found themselves at one of those hastily erected amusement parks that were thrown up outside a local department store. The death-trap Ferris wheel and you-gotta-be-kidding roller coaster provided thrills as far as real life risking of lives and both Quinn and Caesar screamed like there was no tomorrow while Champagne took the whole thing in with an almost blasé indifference. The cotton candy made them all sick. The pizza tasted like it had been microwaved. The white people in their nondescript denim jeans, ridiculous bodily dimensions and sweatshirts of no particular brand were everywhere. They were as much of a source of entertainment as the rides.

Caesar would run into an occasional acquaintance, politely handshaking and patting backs like he was preparing to administer the Heimlich maneuver. Everyone seemed so happy to see him, Quinn noted to herself as he made brief, chatty small talk with each patron before cutting them to ribbons behind their backs to her as soon as they had moved on. She had become so accustomed to people, both men and women who were angry with the world and all the people in it that a man who seemed to be genuinely at peace with himself was a refreshing change.

Now, about the sex…

He touched her and suddenly she felt a charge, probably because it was so unexpected. It was on the inner thigh, which was awkward because a hand has to really work to get to the inner thigh first without stumbling across another part of the anatomy on the way. But it was there: his hand on her inner thigh, very deliberately, almost as if he had aimed. It was shocking, and he was sure that all the gathered white people, who they had both been so thoroughly clowning, must have wondered what had traumatized her as they watched her eyes shoot to wide alert. Her breasts became unbearable, as was always the case when she needed a sexual outlet and there was none available. She almost hated him then for touching her like that. Champagne glanced at her in the middle of all her confusion with a glance far too knowing for that of a five-year-old.

That little bitch! Quinn thought again, as Champagne

looked away laughing before her laughter got choked on a bush of cotton candy she was attempting to swallow. Good for you, Quinn thought, whacking the kid hard across the back till the moistened pink puke nearly jumped out of her throat.

"Thanks," Caesar said dubiously.

"You saved my life," Champagne said, turning wide-eyed to Quinn. "Sort of…"

"No problem," Quinn assured as they walked on to the merry-go-round.

Quinn knew that they were probably too heavy for the ride but she just had to give Caesar a taste of his own medicine, making him ride the same merry-go-round horse as her, only sitting directly behind her. She could feel him growing in his pants as she backed up what little ass she had into him, rubbing and gyrating, up and down and back and forth. He kept adjusting himself in his seat.

"Punk," she said softly, made because he had gotten her all hot and bothered. He rammed his pants-protected erection against her, wrapping his hands around her, right hand over left breast, left hand over right. Quinn was fuming. "If we don't do it tonight, I'm gonna kill you," she said evenly.

"If we don't do it tonight, I'm gonna kill myself," he said in return.

The night began to come. Caesar made it plain that sex at his place was damn near an impossibility being that his mother would be home soon and there was always the issue of Champagne.

"I don't even wanna be around you in a place with beds

if we can't do it," he said slowly in her ear as they got off their fifteenth merry-go-round trip. Quinn nodded. They'd have to wait for Caesar's mother to return so that they could leave Champagne with her, then go running to find someplace to fuck. It was only 8 o'clock. Caesar's mother wouldn't be home till 10. That meant they had two hours to kill.

"Pokemon!" Champagne cheered when asked what movie she wanted to see if the three of them were in fact going to see a movie. *Pokemon*, both Caesar and Quinn though with relief. Good.

It was no use. Despite the complete lack of sex or sexual innuendo, Quinn couldn't help but wanna test the bulge in Caesar's pants as he sat near the wall, she near him and Champagne near her. Quinn's breasts were looking their plumpest too, and Caesar found a way to slip his hand from around her neck to down her T-shirt, turning her nipples like they were the knobs to a hand-held radio. Wanna play rough, huh? Quinn thought to herself, yanking Caesar hard by the base of his shaft once her hand had made it along the path of his stomach towards his member. She couldn't wait to see this thing, still unconvinced but in respectful awe because of the difficulty she was having getting her hands around the thing, remembering how she had always been told she had big fingers for a girl. They were teasing each other, each letting the other get fully aroused, before stopping just short of letting the other climax.

Pokemon was better than either had ever expected.

Caesar's mom was a gruff woman whose humor was

buried to the unintelligent, but Quinn caught herself laughing repeatedly as the woman spoke.

"What are you two getting ready to do?" she asked in a shrill voice that seemed to be going uphill. Both Caesar and Quinn looked guilty as charged. "Oh..." Caesar's mom said when she realized that the question would go unanswered. "Well, have fun," she said with almost an enthusiasm, but Quinn could hear the mockery and she laughed so hard that she wondered if she was being inappropriate.

"I like her," Caesar's mom said to Caesar as he and Quinn were headed out the door.

Two down, Quinn was thinking...

Champagne bragged to her grandmother about the time she'd had with daddy and "Daddy's new girlfriend". The feminist in Quinn had almost cringed audibly with that description of herself. She decided that if she accepted this title that Champagne was more than willing to bestow upon her, the first thing she'd have to do was teach the girl that womanhood was centered, and that a woman could only be a girlfriend, a wife, and even a mother after she was herself first. There were a few more things she could teach the girl too, and it struck her as curious that she found herself wanting to. Every guy she'd ever dated that had kids, their kids had always been *their* kids and, whereas Quinn didn't see herself as ready to adopt Champagne, she could, for a change, see a person in that little girl. A person that could turn out all right.

Caesar and Quinn sat next to each other in the car as it speeded back towards the city. Alone now, they were almost afraid of each other. Neither could speak and the distance from one bucket seat to the other seemed to make each unreachable as each sat at the outside edges of their positions. Both were hoping for a speedy trip to Brooklyn. It took about forty-five minutes, Caesar driving like prize money was being offered. They got out of the car peaceably enough. The even walked to the door of the brownstone as if neither was in any big hurry. But once Quinn reached for the door...

"Hey baby," Maxine called out in the light, choir-like voice she always used to greet Quinn when she hadn't seen her in a while. Luckily, Maxine wasn't looking towards the door. If she had been, she would have seen her daughter being penetrated from behind by a man who was holding her naked breasts while pushing her forward with his pelvis.

"Ma?" Quinn called out, snatching her pants up and her shirt down in one motion. Maxine turned just in time to see her daughter's clothes returning to place and the enormity of Caesar as he stuffed himself back in his pants. She acted like she didn't see the last part.

"Hey girl," Greg said, emerging from the kitchen. He was wearing one of Quinn's bathrobes, tight slacks, black socks, and white sneakers. Quinn's father: always the fashion plate.

"Who's that?" her father asked, regarding Caesar with a bunched up face. "New boyfriend?"

"Uh..." Quinn moaned.

"I hope so," Maxine said under her breath.

"What?" Greg and Quinn asked simultaneously.

"Nothing," Maxine said quickly.

"What are you guys doing here?" Quinn got around to asking.

"Why don't you and your friend come inside, hun?" Maxine asked. Quinn and Caesar both realized that they had been standing inside the doorway. They both walked in.

"Have a seat," Maxine offered Caesar as Quinn went to the kitchen to grab a bottle of spring water.

"Yeah," Greg jumped in. "Let's have a look at you." Caesar obliged, taking a seat in a chair directly across from the sofa. Maxine had already been more than impressed. Greg would not be so easy to please.

"So what do you do, boy?" he asked, before Caesar's seat had grown warm.

"I'm a lab technician at a hospital," he said simply.

"Can you cure AIDS?" Greg asked.

"Don't mind Greg," Maxine began again. "He wants Quinn to marry Al Sharpton."

"Hairdos free for life," Greg chimed in.

"So what brings you two to town?" Quinn asked, returning from the kitchen with two bottles of spring water, one for herself, one for Caesar. He took it thankfully.

"We got news," Greg said flatly.

"Good news," Maxine emphasized.

"What?" Quinn asked.

Greg and Maxine looked at each other, then at Quinn.

"You sure you want us to tell you in front of your company?" Maxine asked.

Quinn frowned.

"What, are you guys getting divorced or something?"

"Kinda the opposite," Greg said.

"What?" Quinn demanded.

Greg and Maxine seemed to take one, unanimous deep breath, then both spoke at once.

"You're gonna be a big sister."

Quinn could feel the rug on her throat, sure her chin had dropped to the floor.

"Aren't you happy?" Maxine asked after a moment had elapsed with no response from Quinn.

"Aren't you old?" Quinn asked almost angrily.

"Quinn," Maxine said, quite hotly herself.

"I'm sorry, mom," Quinn said from a distracted place somewhere in her own mind.

"It's your fault," Greg accused, sounding none too happy, which Quinn knew by now was his way of actually being elated.

"It's nobody's fault," Maxine said patiently, aware that Caesar, the guest, didn't know Greg and might have thought that he was actually disappointed about something both she and his daughter knew him to be thrilled about.

"I think I should be leaving now, Quinn," Caesar said, a voice out of the madness, and Quinn knew for sure, right then, that she loved him.

She watched him as he rose, extending his hand first to her mother and congratulating her, then her father and congratulating him. She watched him further as he approached her, bent and quite correctly pressed a kiss against her cheek as if his thing hadn't just been all up in her not ten minutes before. She watched him as he left without turning back. He would wait. He could wait. He realized that now was not the time.

God, she couldn't believe that she had found this man. A man who understood that a gesture so simple could mean so much. So many other men would have been still pressing her for sex, having experienced just a taste and wanting so desperately to continue that they would have ignored the fact that she had been traumatized by what her family had just told her. Sex was usually such a compulsion for men. She had always known this. Being able to place women in categories, the ones they'd "hit" versus the ones they hadn't and, by conventional standards, it was long past the time that she was supposed to be in Caesar's "hit" category. But she wasn't yet, and he would wait. What that said about him was even more than that little bit of sex she had gotten at the door. And that little bit of sex had said a lot.

He'd been decisive about it too. It wasn't as if he'd asked. He'd just decided to leave and left. God, how long she'd wanted a man who could make his own decisions and follow them out like that. The truth was, she hadn't been really traumatized. The issue of her parents becoming parents again at their age had struck her more as comedy than anything else. She imagined that she'd be doing more raising of the baby then they would. Lord knew, as out of touch with everything as they were about her own generation, they'd be double out of touch when the baby came. Hell, they still thought Run DMC was the top rap group.

But back to Caesar, and that's where her mind kept returning for the remainder of the night. As Maxine and Greg slept quietly in her bed and she slept on the futon in the living room, her thoughts kept returning to him like a boomerang. How beautiful he was. How strong. How big his... well, she didn't really linger there too long because it caused her to begin to play with herself and she was at the point now where having witnessed the kind of control he'd demonstrated, she didn't want to feel like the weak one in the relationship. She rubbed her stomach instead. And dredlocked her pubic hairs just a little.

"I'm so happy for you," Carmen's words said the next day and if Quinn hadn't been so intuitive, she would have taken them at face value and that would have been the end of it. But Quinn knew better. Carmen's eyes were hollowed and red. Her nose was red too. Her hair was pulled back in a bun. And she was wearing a dress. Not a skirt. A dress. A peasant dress like one would imagine on a Spanish senorita of old, chaste in either virginity or mourning and just as neurotic.

"Thank you," Quinn said, looking at her friend a little harder and wondering why it had taken so long to notice what seemed to be so evident now. She had been at work for nearly two hours. She had initially taken Carmen's silence not as an attitude, but as a choice. A person had a right to be quiet on occasion, even Carmen. But it had taken mentioning Caesar, her parents and the night before, telling Carmen that she thought she'd done it, she thought she'd found 'The One' before she realized that Carmen was so far away from her right then, the best she could give were surface responses.

And when she said "I'm so happy for you," there were tears. Tears that only a fool would have mistaken as tears of joy. Quinn felt like a heel. She walked across the floor towards her friend. When she arrived, she took Carmen by the hand and held it. She kissed her softly on the cheek.

"What's wrong?" she asked in a voice as soft as a mother's.

"Oh Quinn…" Carmen broke, her words being choked by tears that were more evident.

"Me and Steeze broke up," she said, when she could speak again.

Quinn's heart sank to the floor.

"Aw baby," she pleaded, using her free hand to stroke the back of Carmen's neck. "What happened?"

"I told him the truth," Carmen said simply.

Quinn was confused.

"The truth?" she asked.

"About me and all those other men."

Quinn quickly became enraged.

"You mean with all the pussy that mothafucka was getting he got mad 'cause you got some dick after he agreed to it?" she asked incredulously.

Carmen shook her head and began sobbing harder.

"No," Carmen moaned, still shaking her head. "That was a lie." Quinn was confused again. "There were no other men," Carmen continued. "I just told Steeze that so he'd wanna stop fooling around. I never slept with another man the entire time that we were together. I told him that yesterday and he left me."

Quinn closed her eyes tight and shook her head as if she was trying to force the evil thoughts that filled it to flee.

"You mean he left you 'cause you weren't cheating on him?" Quinn asked, about as incredulous as she had ever been.

Carmen nodded in her arms. Quinn shook her head again.

"He said the guilt would be too much for him. And that eventually he knew he'd have to pay for what he'd done to me, since I hadn't done anything to him. "I want him back, Quinn," Carmen wailed, the words slicing Quinn open like razors. She exhaled, hard.

"Come by my house tonight," she said to Carmen simply. "I have an idea that might help."

Quinn was happy that her parents had left. They were actually on one of their goodwill tours during which they swept through the northeastern states visiting family and friends bringing peace and love. Well, in her mother's case, peace and love. In her father's case, temper tantrums and obnoxious jokes. But they did have good news this time. Maxine would be a mother again, and Quinn could only imagine the kind of pressure that must have been putting on her parent's male friends. If it was anything like Shortie's pregnancy had made her feel, then there were a lot of old women having more sex than they'd had in years.

She had talked to Caesar for about an hour that day before she forced herself to get off the phone. He told her that Champagne liked her. She almost hated herself for being happy about the fact. Caesar told her about a party that was happening that Friday that he himself had heard about from that asshole: Phil Flarn. She felt herself acutely out of the loop, hearing about a party in Manhattan from a dude in New London, New York. She said she'd go, though. She might as well go. Caesar was going, she thought with a smile. It was always so sexy to be at a party with a boy and not looking for one. Something about a satisfied woman was like an aphrodisiac to boys, whereas a desperate woman was like a boy repellent. Caesar would be good arm candy too, Quinn thought. His pretty-ass eyes and slim physique. Plus, he hadn't been through the 'circuit' of her friends and neighbors, having had sex with everybody she knew, herself being the most recent. 'Circuit' guys were always the last resort of the truly desperate. If anything, Quinn had always preferred to be the one that had started a guy on the 'circuit' as opposed to picking up one that was already out there. And with any luck at all, Caesar would never hit the 'circuit'.

Quinn stepped outside her apartment and came back in. The smell of the incense was strong. The candle light cast the sort of atmosphere that she herself would like to be seduced in and she could imagine giving in to just about anything in a room like this. She thought about drugs. It had been such a while since she had done anything, even weed. God knew, at one point her daily ritual had been a blunt for breakfast, one for lunch, one for dinner, and a half of one just so she could sleep. For some reason, the events of her life almost ever since she had met Caesar had made her forget about drugs. Maybe it was some perceived purity about him? She didn't know. All she knew was that she hadn't had anything so she hadn't wanted anything. But now she needed something. All of her old contacts had changed numbers, them being the type of people constantly on the go for fear of being caught up with. She thought of Life. There was no way that she could call him now and he had the best shit. She panicked for a second, then she calmed again and thought.

The drummer.

"Trent?" she asked into the phone.

"Who's this, Quinn?" the drummer asked.

"Yeah."

"What, girl?"

"I need a favor."

"I'm not donating no sperm, Quinn," the drummer mocked.

"Stop playing. I need you to call Life and get me some Ex and some weed."

"Why can't you call him?"

" 'Cause I can't." There was a pause.

"I suppose you want me to deliver it too," the drummer asked, only then his voice slipping into the kind of cadence that might have suggested that he liked the fellahs.

"Yeah," Quinn said sheepishly.

"Then you need three favors," the drummer quipped. "Contact, purchase and delivery."

"Yeah," Quinn moaned.

"I better get some dick from this," the drummer said.

"The next hot gay guy I meet," Quinn promised.

He was hot, Quinn thought when the drummer arrived at the door bearing gifts. She could see why Shortie had fucked him. He was as ugly as a monkey and carried himself as if his was the only way to look. She had half a mind to ask him to pull it out. She had heard so much about it, but she thought of Caesar and paused, then frowned. She would have actually considered herself cheating on Caesar if she had asked to see the drummer's dick. She wondered how she felt about what was going to happen later on that night.

"Let me come in and smoke with you, girl," the drummer demanded, pushing Quinn aside as he stormed into her apartment and sought a place to camp. Quinn watched him through a bunched-up expression, aware that his request was the least thing she could do considering all that he had done for her. He took a seat on her futon, split open a cigar and began building a blunt expertly. They smoked in silence.

Quinn's mind began to fade. She thought of Caesar and how she would explain if called to explain about her actions tonight. It wasn't cheating, she'd say. She loved Carmen. She wondered if he'd go for it. She wondered, moreover, if she'd go for it if he explained that he'd had sex with some man that he loved. The more she thought about it, the guiltier she felt.

"What's wrong with you?" the drummer asked, noticing the look on Quinn's face.

"Nothing," she said, shaking her head to mirror the word.

"Bullshit nothing," the drummer said, taking a puff then looking away towards the window. "You got somebody on your mind."

Quinn sucked her teeth.

"I'm about to do something tonight," she said after a pregnant pause.

"Something you don't want to do?" the drummer asked.

"Yeah," Quinn offered weakly.

"Then don't do it," the drummer offered definitively.

Quinn sucked her teeth again.

"It's not that simple," she said.

"Why not?" the drummer asked.

"Because it's for a friend," she said simply.

The drummer looked at her, incredulous.

"Bitch, you had me get out of my warm bed to call your ex-man, then come over here to bring you some drugs and you're worried about how you treat a friend? I guess I ain't your friend, huh?"

"It's not like that."

"What's it like then?"

There was a knock at the door.

Quinn rushed to it, forgetting what was on the other side, eager to escape this conversation with the drummer.

Carmen looked quite intrigued, actually. She looked like she might have, in fact, suspected what Quinn had in mind. And she was down. The thought both relieved Quinn and make her uneasy. There was suddenly more pressure because there was less. The weed was making her crazy.

"Isn't that the dude who came into the store with Phil Flarn that day?" Carmen asked, peeping over Quinn's shoulder. It was then Quinn realized that she hadn't yet invited Carmen inside and that from where she was standing in the doorway, Carmen could see all the way over to the futon and the drummer.

"Yeah, that's Trent," Quinn said a little uncomfortably.

"Trent the drummer?" Carmen asked.

Quinn frowned for a minute, forgetting that not only had Carmen seen the drummer in person, but Quinn had described for her Shortie and Dred and the drummer's fiasco. Now Carmen was reconciling the name with the face.

"Yeah," Quinn said. "That's him."

"Can I come in?" Carmen asked. Quinn opened the door wide enough for an elephant to pass through. "Hi, I'm Carmen," she said, almost racing over to the drummer. He smirked, extending a hand.

Quinn shook her head, taking the whole thing in. Look at him sitting there like he's the bitch, she thought to herself. People got away with what they could, she guessed.

"I remember you," the drummer said, his sweet side showing. "And girl, you got an ass on you that would make my dick hard."

Carmen turned eagerly, whipping up her oversized sweatshirt, happy to flash that thing before him.

"Ooh," he moaned, grabbing himself.

Quinn just shook her head. At this point, anything seemed possible.

"I heard stories about you too," Carmen cheered. "About your dick. Can I see it?"

The drummer stood up. He was wearing button-fly jeans, Quinn guessed to make a potential situation like this, a call for his undressing, all the more dramatic. The drummer began to unbutton his fly. Quinn watched with a sort of unsteady eye, looking, but not really watching. Then he had his pants fully unbuttoned.

Now, she had felt Caesar's dick. It was about as big as a ketchup bottle. Bigger than almost anything she had ever seen, felt, or experienced in her life. But as the drummer began to uncoil his member, inch by inch, by inch, there was a point at which Quinn stopped believing in reality.

"Stop!" she cried, unwilling to believe that the thing nearly touching the ground was inanimate.

"Ooooooh," Carmen moaned, to herself this time, as if witnessing something too pretty for words. She whipped off her sweatshirt, turned back around and snatched down her stretch pants.

"Can you rub it on me?" she asked the drummer. He grabbed himself by the base and began caressing the crack of her behind with his shaft. He slowly grew hard. Carmen reached back and grabbed him by the arm, pulling him close to her.

"Rub my body," she whispered.

He began rubbing from the bottom of her breasts to her pelvis, back and forth, up and down. The direction of the thing changed to the point where it was nearly touching the drummer's chin.

"Put it in," Carmen moaned.

The drummer took a few steps back and Carmen bent forward, then slowly, carefully, began inserting himself.

Quinn watched the whole thing in dumb shock. The drummer was fucking Carmen. And it looked like it was good. She didn't know whether to be happy or jealous. Sure, now she wasn't gonna have to cheat on Caesar, but a part of her couldn't deny that she was a bit upset that now she'd never get to have sex with Carmen. She decided to take some Ex instead.

Fifteen minutes later, she was masturbating to the sight

of both of them. Carmen and that vastly ranging ass that bounced and rebounded along the drummer's pelvis. The drummer, expertly wielding the enormous machinery that hung from him. It was quite sexy actually. And it lasted for quite a while. Quinn probably came more times than either of the participants had. In the end, they all shared a smoke.

Quinn slept alone, thinking again of Caesar. She was happy that she hadn't done anything that she would have later regretted. It was so hard for her to give straight bets relationship-wise. She was so used to guys who couldn't hold up their end of the deal that she had long ago begun a practice of committing the first infraction, so when the guy's turn came around to fuck up, she'd already done her dirt. But this time with Caesar would be different she promised herself. She would actually allow herself to be vulnerable again. And if in the end, he turned out to be a jerk, well, at least she'd have known that she gave it the best that she had.

Carmen was back to normal the next day at work even though they went the whole day without talking about the events of the night before. It wasn't as if either had much to say about it. They had both been there. Every once in a while though one would look up and catch the other looking at her and smiling and have to crack a smile and giggle in return. This went on all day. Before the end of the day, Bill had come downstairs. He was just standing around looking silly, so Quinn and Carmen did what they could to ignore him. They knew he had spent just about the entire day jacking off. He could only look either of them in the eye once his body had been emptied of all desire.

"So what's the deal, Quinn?" he asked, like he was her friend or something.

She looked at him like he was a stranger on the street posing the same question.

"I heard about you turning down that deal with Alanda," he continued, undeterred. Now she looked interested. He smiled knowingly. "Staying true to your art, huh?" he asked.

Quinn frowned bitterly, shaking her head quickly.

"I just don't wanna sing R&B," she said, dismissive.

"Wanna sing jazz?" Bill said.

Quinn looked confused.

"You telling me or asking me?" she asked.

"Asking."

"Sure."

Bill nodded.

"I'm doing the new soundtrack and I want you to be on it for real," he said seriously. "And that's not just because I'm your boss here or 'cause I've seen you and Carmen engaging in lesbian sex."

Quinn frowned.

"That's 'cause I've heard some of your stuff," Bill continued. "And I think you're good. Real good."

"Thanks Bill," Quinn said sincerely.

"I want you to come by my studio on 23rd Street in the city next Wednesday and check out this jazz band I've been working with. Only thing is, they need a drummer. Know any?"

Quinn and Carmen cast each other knowing glances.

"What's this I hear about all the pussy you've been getting lately?" that asshole: Phil Flarn's voice was the first that she heard as she walked in the door of the club. He was standing seemingly right up under the entrance, holding the drummer captive against the wall. Quinn had walked in hand-in-hand with Caesar. He had picked her up from work that day and they had gone out to dinner. Now it was time to party, sort of. She looked from Phil Flarn over to the drummer just in time to see him shrug.

"You been looking at Joyce funny?" Phil Flarn asked, as the drummer shook his head in mock terror. He looked over his own shoulder to notice Quinn and Caesar entering. "What's up Quinn?" Phil Flarn asked. "What's up Caese? I heard about that dick of yours," Phil Flarn continued. "And I don't want it anywhere near me or any of my family…"

Quinn and Caesar wandered deeper into the crowd. It was Caesar's type of place, him being one for well-lit spots with oversized, way too colorful lounge furniture and people who looked like they just escaped from purgatory. Quinn, much more familiar with that particular scene, was unimpressed. What did impress her however was that this seemed to be the same party that she had met Caesar at, just in a different location. It had almost all the same people, then some. Caesar stopped to order drinks for them at the bar. Quinn walked off alone towards the back of the place. Alanda jumped out at her from behind a pillar.

"Heard you're gonna be on Bill's new soundtrack," she

said as eagerly as if she was telling good news about herself.

Quinn started to frown, but fought through it.

"Yeah," she said, forcing a smile, wondering how on earth Alanda knew about that.

"We really need to get together," Alanda was saying. "Sit down and talk."

"Yeah," was all that Quinn could say before she started looking away, looking for somewhere to go to get away from this girl. The men were hot and heavy on her. Her breasts seemed to be like magnets, attracting the eyes and seemingly using gravity to pull the most eerie assortment of men that she had ever seen gathered together in one place. And it wasn't that any of them were speaking to her. They were just approaching, drinks in hand, eyes tit level, staring as if waiting for her to say something. When it rained, it poured. When Quinn had been hungry for a man or for somebody promising a recording deal, nobody had been anywhere to be found. Now that she had Caesar at her side and Bill waiting for her the following Wednesday, Alanda and these creepy-ass men were everywhere. She suddenly regretted the fact that she had come. That is, until she saw Carmen and Steeze. They came bouncing up, hand-in-hand like a pair of goofy white teenagers from one of those 1950s movies.

"What are y'all doing here?" Quinn asked, aware that this wasn't Carmen's usual partying crowd, though not surprised at all about seeing the two of them together as a couple again. She had known they would be. She loved being right.

"I wanted to come," Carmen said quickly, eager to demonstrate who was now calling the shots in the relationship.

Quinn nodded appreciatively. She looked near the door. Joyce had just walked in. That asshole: Phil Flarn grabbed her immediately and pulled her away from the drummer who she was on her way to hug, hollering, "Stand back!" at the top of his lungs.

Caesar approached Quinn, Carmen and Steeze carrying the drinks. And when she looked at him, looked at his mouth and the way his lips were slightly parted, looked in his eyes and the way they were wide open and taking in everything, suddenly she couldn't wait to get him home.

Caesar had been long gone. Quinn had actually gotten out of bed, but returned. She missed the bed. His smell was still in it. She had almost asked him to leave something. His wife-beater T-shirt or a sock, something with his person more definitively defined, but she had stopped just short. She settled for his smell. It was an honest smell. One of soap, light sweat, deodorant and soul. Black soul. Sorta like black love. Quinn felt so corny, rolling around in her bed, soaking up a man's smell. Still, she couldn't think of anything better to do. She thought how much had happened since she had met Caesar. It was funny, she had known she could sing the whole time, but it was as if now, only for the first time, she felt comfortable with the knowledge. She wasn't in a rush about it. She was settled. She had always felt like her whole life had been passing her by even as she was living it. She had always had this terrible tendency of valuing herself versus the accomplishments of others. Mary J. Blige was the same age as her and was world famous. Shit, Lauryn Hill was even younger. But now, Quinn felt blessed. Blessed to have lived the life she led. Who knew what price those famous people had paid for their fame? Who knew what the true cost had been? In her own defense, Quinn did have her regrets, but they were regrets caused by her own missteps, not missteps taken following someone else in the wrong direction.

Quinn breathed a deep exhale, her hand finding itself right beneath her breasts as she lay on her back. What a life she had lived. And it was just beginning, she thought with a smile. There was a song to do on Wednesday, work to do always, and Caesar. Yes, now there was Caesar. And who knew? Maybe he wouldn't last. Maybe none of it would. Maybe tomorrow oblivion would come, Caesar would turn out to be as gay as the drummer or as big an asshole as Phil Flarn. Maybe Bill would change his mind about the record, Alanda would stop talking about a record deal and, shit, maybe even her parents would want to move back to New York, want their place back, and kick her out on the street. Maybe she'd lose her job at Big Niggaz, be forced to turn to prostitution and contract a venereal disease that turned her insides into a kumquat.

She laughed. Who ever knew what the future held, she thought, looking over at the table and seeing a big, fat, half-smoked blunt laying crooked across an ashtray. She debated for a moment with the idea of puffing it a little, but the idea lost. She decided to remain smoke-free for a day and, if that worked, try it again tomorrow. In fact, that was how she now decided to live her life. Go with what works. Caesar was making her feel good right now so, if she could, she'd go with Caesar again tomorrow. Not smoking was making her feel good right now, so if she continued to feel good, she wouldn't smoke or do any Ex tomorrow. Realistically, God was making her feel good and the thought sobered her a little because she felt that she had been taking too much credit for all the things in her life that were suddenly going right.

"Thank you God," she said, dropping to her knees in almost one motion from being flat on her back on the bed.

She felt better. She decided that she'd make doing that a routine at least once a day. Everything suddenly seemed good. She was happy for her mother and father because of the baby. Shit, she was even happy for Shortie. She was happy that Carmen and Steeze had gotten back together. She was happy for Joyce and that asshole: Phil Flarn. She was happy that Bill was about to make another movie. She was happy that she was going to be on the soundtrack. She was happy that it was Saturday and she didn't have to work that day. She was happy that the sun was shinning. Lastly, she was happy that she had met Caesar and that they had spent one of the best nights she had ever experienced in her entire life together the night before. The only thing she wasn't happy about was that he was gone. She picked up the phone to call him.

"Yes?" Champagne's voice asked over the line.

Quinn shook her head. How that child could use a young woman as a role model...

"Let me speak to your father, Champagne."

"Daddy, it's for you…" Champagne said, a giggle running hot through her voice.

"Hello?" Caesar said, his voice always shockingly deeper over the phone than it was in person. Or did it just seem different because you could see him, Quinn wondered. He looked like a pretty boy. His face and body certainly didn't match his voice. Neither did his dick.

"Hello?" Caesar asked again forcing Quinn to realize that she had been thinking, not speaking.

"Hello yourself," she said, sounding about as sexy as the first kiss after an orgasm. He breathed a chuckle that was almost girly, except that it was deep. "Happy to hear from me?" she mocked.

"About as happy as you are to call," he said evenly. Quinn wrinkled her lips.

"Well, I'm very happy to call," she said quickly.

"And I'm very happy to hear from you," he said just as quickly.

So we're gonna play this game, Quinn thought. The, "I'm only as open off of you as you are off of me" game. To be honest, she was a little disappointed. But after all, what we she expecting? So what if he was fine, funny, smart, warm, ate pussy better than Shortie and fucked better than Life, he was still just a man. And just that quickly she started falling out of love with him. She felt she was already beginning to know his boundaries. She could punk him by putting him on the spot. She decided to end the games right there by putting him on a spot he certainly couldn't return from.

"So when are you and Champagne moving down to Brooklyn?" she asked, ready for him to stumble on his words.

"I was just looking through the newspaper for available apartments today," he said without missing a beat.

Quinn's side of the line went dead silent.

"Hello?" Caesar asked, to no response from Quinn.

"Hello?" he asked again.

END